Her nostrils flared at the intense metallic aroma permeating through the room and awakening her sleepy senses. She tucked her knees to her chest and cloaked them with the front of Mark's oversized shirt for a little added warmth.

"Mark, do you smell that? I think we have a gas leak or something."

Sniffing again, this time deeper, she scuttled back against his warm body and closed her eyes, removing her legs from inside the shirt and wrapping her ankles around his like a boa constrictor.

The floor had numbed most of her body, so she wiggled from one side to the other until she regained feeling. They must've slept on the floor all night. Ten years ago, her body would've recovered easily, but now she'd be sore and stiff for at least a week.

She reached behind her and patted his stomach. "Mark?"

A warm, thick liquid coated her arm and hand. She lifted her head and bent her arm.

Rays of sunlight illuminated the shimmering crimson racing down her wrist like wax down a burning candle.

Blood.

Secluded

by

D. M. Grant

Small Town Sins, Book One

Secluded

Cover Art by *Diana Carlile*

The Wild Rose Press, Inc.
PO Box 708
Adams Basin, NY 14410-0708
Visit us at www.thewildrosepress.com

Publishing History
First Edition, 2023
Trade Paperback ISBN 978-1-5092-4902-2
Digital ISBN 978-1-5092-4903-9

Small Town Sins, Book One
Published in the United States of America

Dedication

To my family for encouraging and believing in me.

To my beta readers, Kari, Kayla, Sarah, and Barb, for wading through my dreadful drafts.

To Alex, my editor, for taking a chance on my book and me.

Chapter One

Ugh.

A drum solo pounded in her head, worsening as she lifted her back off the floor, and her mouth felt cottony.

What the hell happened last night?

Sunlight swept across the floor, illuminating the two half-full glasses of burgundy wine on the coffee table.

Mark brought the imported Italian wine home for their anniversary last night, and she had the honor of popping the cork herself. If they didn't even finish one glass, why couldn't she remember anything after the first sip? She was a lightweight, but not that light.

Chilled, she brushed her hands across her chest and gripped nothing but bare flesh, only adding to the pile of unanswered questions. The white button-down crumpled on the floor beside her would have to suffice until she could make it to the bedroom.

Some leggings and a hoodie would be a godsend right about now.

She thrust her arms into the sleeves and pushed her head through the neck hole. The fabric rubbed against her goose bumps, and a shiver ran from her spine to her toes. Her head throbbed with every movement.

Her nostrils flared at the intense metallic aroma permeating through the room and awakening her sleepy senses. She tucked her knees to her chest and cloaked them with the front of Mark's oversized shirt for a little added warmth.

"Mark, do you smell that? I think we have a gas leak or something."

Sniffing again, this time deeper, she scuttled back against his warm body and closed her eyes, removing her legs from inside the shirt and wrapping her ankles around his like a boa constrictor.

The floor had numbed most of her body, so she wiggled from one side to the other until she regained feeling. They must've slept on the floor all night. Ten years ago, her body would've recovered easily, but now she'd be sore and stiff for at least a week.

She reached behind her and patted his stomach. "Mark?"

A warm, thick liquid coated her arm and hand. She lifted her head and bent her arm.

Rays of sunlight illuminated the shimmering crimson racing down her wrist like wax down a burning candle.

Blood.

Her stomach churned, and bile rose to the back of her throat. She rolled over and slid away, twisting toward the source. Nothing could've prepared her for the gory river, the empty, lifeless eyes, or the countless slashes in her husband's chest.

"What the hell?"

She had to be dreaming. She must be stuck in some type of hypnagogic hallucination or something. Taking a sliver of skin between her thumb and pointer finger, she squeezed hard.

Ow! Her theory now thoroughly shattered, she

screamed into the silent air.

A squeak followed by a soft click echoed from the kitchen.

She stood, fumbling toward the noise, wobbly from sleeping on a hardwood floor with no cushion.

Almost there.

Just a few more steps.

She yanked the cordless phone from its cradle and dialed 9-1-1.

Crisp fall air seeped into the kitchen from the wide-open the back door.

She had locked that door, she was sure of it.

Someone else had been there, in their home, without being noticed. They'd just witnessed the entire scene in the living room unfold, probably admiring their handiwork.

The burning knot in her stomach rose violently. Anything lingering in her system was expelled across the new linoleum flooring Mark had just installed.

The line rang, and the grandfather clock *ticked* and *tocked* loyally from the corner while she used the back of her hand to wipe putrid saliva from her lips. "Come on, isn't anyone going to answer the fuc—

"911, what's your emergency?"

"Please send help! I need someone to help me right now!"

"Ma'am, calm down. Take a deep breath, and as clearly as you can, tell me your name and exactly what happened."

"M-my name is Halley Martin. I-I don't know what happened, but it's my husband. He's been stabbed or something, and he's not breathing!"

"Okay. We're sending help right away. What's

your address?"

"It's, uh…" She'd lived in the same house for the past ten years, and yet somehow, the Goddamn address eluded her. "I-I can't remember the numbers, but it's the first house on Briarwood. Please hurry."

"I've dispatched the closest unit. They're on the way. Have you started CPR? If you don't know how, I'll walk you through the steps."

She'd done CPR before…once, but it'd been years ago. More importantly, starting chest compressions hadn't occurred to her until the operator said something. What kind of wife finds her husband bloodied and not breathing but doesn't try to do something immediately? "No. I can do it. I can do this."

Halley dropped the phone. She crawled back to Mark, her trembling legs unable to support her weight any longer. Her eyes stung. How much time had gone by since she'd last blinked?

Cementing herself beside Mark's motionless body, she studied him. The blue-jay color that once inhabited his irises was now muddled and raw. The warm, inviting light that used to occupy them, gone—erased without reason, rendering them cold and colorless.

Her subconscious reason for not beginning chest compressions was now crystal clear. Mark was gone, and nothing she did would bring him back. But if she didn't try, she might always wonder. Miracles had happened before. Not to her, but they'd happened.

Halley placed the palms of her hands on Mark's still-warm chest, careful not to press on any of the open wounds. Blood seeped from the closest slice, which turned into a hole when she pressed down. Her fingers disappeared beneath the liquid pooling at the center of his chest, painted a red so deep they almost turned black. She repeated the motion thirty times, then pried open his mouth and blew two deep breaths into his body.

The last time she saw her mother's face flashed as she released the last breath. Just like that, she was twenty years in the past, begging her mom to wake up, pounding on her chest with clenched fists that were halfway between a woman's and a child's.

The too-familiar scene stilled her. She'd locked away the past, but her psyche found the hidden key.

Halley blinked away the memory. She had to focus, to continue CPR until the ambulance arrived. The point of no return had long since passed, but no one would be able to say she didn't try.

****

The police radio sounded. "Calling all units. Unresponsive male in the first house on Briarwood. Please respond."

That couldn't be right. The first house on Briarwood was Mark and Halley's. The dispatcher must've made a mistake. "This is Officer Jared Collins. Are you positive about the location?"

"That is correct," the dispatcher said.

"Okay. I'm en route."

Jared whipped the car around, narrowly avoiding a collision, and flicked on his flashing lights. The unresponsive male had to be Mark, but he was in great shape, and they were the same age. What in the hell could've possibly caused him to become unresponsive?

"Is everything all right? Do you know whose house that is?" Bo Frazer, Jared's partner, tilted his head to the side and frowned.

"Yeah. It's my friend, Mark, and his wife, Halley's, place." Jared didn't say that Mark had been his friend since childhood, and they grew up right next door to one another. Mark was more a brother than a friend.

"I remember you mentioning them before. Mark's not that old, is he? I thought you guys were the same age."

"We are."

Jared pulled into the driveway. "Follow me in, but lag behind a bit until I figure out what's going on." He was built for this job, and he'd always been confident when entering a crime scene, but this time was different—something wasn't right.

His heart raced, and sweaty palms messed with the grip he had on his gun. He stopped short of the open back door and lowered his weapon, wiping the sweat on his pants.

Booking the bad guy was what kept Jared in uniform—not to mention the satisfaction he obtained from a good ole adrenaline rush. Nine times out of ten, though, the victims were nameless, holding no significant attachment for him in a personal capacity...until now.

Jared peered in through the cracked window blinds. If he could just catch a glimpse of Halley or Mark, he'd be able to calm down—to put his racing thoughts into perspective.

"Halley?" A soft, feminine whimper floated through the screen door, but he received no answer. He spoke again, louder this time. "Halley, it's me, Jared. Are you in there?" Still nothing. "Okay. If you aren't going to answer me, then stay where you are. I'm coming in."

The overwhelming scent of blood hit him hard when he entered the kitchen. Personal experience had scarred him. Where there's lots of blood, there's usually death.

He shifted his grip on his gun, only breathing when necessary, and he craned his neck, motioning for Bo to follow.

"Jesus. That's a pretty strong smell. Maybe I should go in first."

Jared waved him away. "Back off, Bo. I can handle whatever is in there." He passed through the mahogany archway dividing the kitchen and living room.

Dark-red dots scattered across the stones cemented into the fireplace, and small streams of blood had crept under the blanket laid out on the floor and pooled in the crevices. The ghastly scene far surpassed every scenario his imagination had conjured.

Ten years on the police force had prepared him for the harsh realities of life and death but neglected to prime him for how to react when the situation became personal—when a person he cared about was stretched out on a blanket, naked and soaked in blood.

Halley huddled beside Mark with her knees pulled tight to her chest. Tears streamed down her face as she stared at the floor, and streaks of blood covered almost every inch of her.

Jared holstered his gun and moved toward Halley. "Bo, check for a pulse." He knelt and lowered his voice to just over a whisper. "Halley, are you all right?" When she didn't bother to look at or answer him, he crept closer and lifted her chin so he could look into her eyes. "You need to answer me. Are you hurt anywhere?"

Halley locked onto his gaze. "Mark's dead."

Halley's words startled him. Mark's body was on the floor right in front of him, but wasn't there a possibility—even a small one—he could pull through? What was he thinking? He counted at least a dozen stab wounds at a glance, but there were probably more.

Scratch that…there were *always* more.

Mark's eyes were open, and his mouth hung open.

Still, Jared needed confirmation. He turned to Bo and cleared his throat.

Bo twisted at the hip, his gaze never leaving the ground, and shook his head.

Damn. The blow hit as a strange mixture of both surprise and acceptance. In a split second, Bo had severed Jared's last thread of hope for his friend.

He leaned over his best friend, his brother. If he could've screamed out loud, every window in that house would have shattered across the floor in a million tiny shards. Why would anyone want to kill Mark? He was a husband, an engineer, and a friend, not the type of person people usually set out to murder.

Bo grabbed Jared's shoulder, ripping him away from the ramblings in his mind.

"Do you want to call the coroner, or should I?"

Jared closed Mark's eyelids and stood. "You call the coroner, and I'll call the captain."

Bo nodded, turned, exited through the archway, and disappeared into the kitchen.

Enough was enough. Halley had to know what happened. She had to have been there when the murder took place, so she must've seen something. He'd get the truth, even if he had to shake a statement out of her.

Reaching under Halley's arms, he lifted her off the floor to her feet.

"Look at me." She did, and he stared into her blue-green eyes. The lights were on, but nobody was home. "I'm gonna walk you to the kitchen table, and you're going to tell me everything that happened between yesterday and today. Do you understand?"

She nodded, but he couldn't be sure if she grasped what he said, so he shook her shoulders. "Do you?"

Halley's eyes widened.

Jared had just done the unthinkable, and reality settled into his gut like a gas station sandwich. He steadied her and loosened his grip. How could he have handled her so rough? She seemed to be in shock, and he'd made things ten times worse for her.

The badge pinned to his shirt didn't put him above the law; yet for a moment, he'd forgotten, or maybe he truly believed otherwise. "I'm so sorry. I had no right to shake you like that."

What was wrong with him? What if he had shaken her too hard? What if he hadn't been able to stop? The real question lingered in the dark crevices of his mind—why was he acting like his father? As he was growing up, showing anger meant one thing…someone would pay a painful price.

Years of counseling and hard work were supposed to help squelch his rage. Nobody was going to get hurt on his watch—especially not by his hand.

Jared guided her to the couch. An unfamiliar feeling washed over him. Tingling started in his hands, spreading to the rest of his limbs. His breathing quickened, and everything around him began to spin. He needed to get some air before he passed out.

Jared ran past Bo at full speed, practically bursting through the kitchen screen door. Air filled his lungs. He slid his back down the vinyl siding and buried his head between his legs. Becoming a cop was supposed to teach him control—to rein in his emotions—but the man he saw reflected in Halley's eyes was unrecognizable. And she was the one person he never wanted to hurt.

He took an oath ten years ago to serve and protect. In the living room, with Halley, he did neither one of those things. He fiddled with the metal shield pinned to his shirt. Maybe he didn't deserve to wear the clunky piece of metal after all.

The cell phone in his pocket vibrated. When he looked down, Captain Maxwell's number danced across the screen. Jared took a deep breath and raised the phone to his ear. "Hello, Captain. I was just getting ready to call you."

"Collins. Fill me in."

Captain Lawrence Maxwell was a fair man, but he never strayed far from the book. Ever since his second daughter started looking at colleges, he'd been even more pissy than usual. If Jared's connection to Mark and Halley came to the man's attention, he'd be yanked from the case faster than a cheetah running down dinner. *For now, just tell the captain what he wanted to hear and leave the details to a minimum.*

"Uh, we have a deceased, thirty-year-old male with multiple stab wounds to his chest and abdomen. The ambulance hasn't arrived yet, but I had Bo call the coroner anyway. I need you to notify homicide and send a forensics team out here. I'm about to see what info I can obtain from the wife."

"Was she there when the possible homicide took place? Is she a suspect?"

He'd never thought of that. It seemed far-fetched, but so did losing his best friend to murder.

What if she had a hand in it? Or, worse yet, what if she stabbed him all on her own?

If Halley had anything to do with Mark's death, Jared would find out. Personal feelings aside, Mark's killer could be standing in the living room as the captain droned on. It happened more often than people liked to believe.

"I honestly don't know, sir. She's not really talking at the moment. I think she's in shock."

"Well, what exactly are you waiting for, Collins? Get a statement and bring her ass down. If you can't get any useful information out of her, then I'll find someone else who can."

The phone went silent.

Once Jared dropped Halley off at the station, she'd be out of his hands. He was an officer, not a detective, and they'd take over tornado-style—quick and without much warning. Sure, she might be a cold-blooded killer, but Halley was still his friend, and that had to count for something, right?

Chapter Two

Halley jolted at the knock on the front door. Nobody ever came in through the front of the house unless a salesperson who happened to be working the area was selling unnecessary crap or someone's car broke down nearby. Sometimes she forgot the entrance even existed.

Jared's partner—Bo something—walked down the narrow hallway, put his eye to the peephole, and opened the door.

She'd overheard Jared mention his newest partner to Mark the last time he came for dinner, but he never gave a last name.

Halley craned her neck and peeked around the corner.

Two paramedics stood at the entrance, and Bo glanced over his shoulder before turning his back to her.

He spoke in hushed tones, but she could still hear every exchange between them.

"The body is over there by the fireplace. You can try CPR if you need to, but…" Bo lowered his voice even more.

She shifted slightly so she'd have a better shot at hearing their conversation, but all she heard was, "…he doesn't have a pulse."

Halley sat quietly on the couch as the paramedics,

one of whom looked like she wasn't old enough to drive, set up their workspace.

The middle-aged man with a receding hairline began chest compressions, while the young woman with her bouncing ponytail blew breaths into Mark's mouth.

Maybe it was protocol, but Halley'd already done this. How long were they going to keep working on him before they called it?

Enough was enough.

"Stop." Halley cleared her dry throat, swallowing the small amount of saliva she had left. "I said, 'stop'." Her voice gained more volume, but they still didn't hear her.

A deafening *crack* rang out from beneath the paramedic's hands.

"Stop, Goddammit! You're breaking him." They heard her for sure that time.

Both paramedics' heads snapped up at the sound of her voice.

She rose from the couch and hobbled toward them. "Don't you think I already tried that?"

The female paramedic stood in front of her. "Ma'am, I know that must've sounded awful, but broken or cracked ribs sometimes happen when we do compressions. I promise he didn't feel any pain."

"No shit, he didn't feel any pain, you idiot. He's fucking dead!"

The young woman's eyes widened.

Halley's chest heaved. There wasn't enough air. She needed more air. She stiffened her body tighter than a rubber band and clenched her fists.

She unfurled her right hand and swung it out to the

side just behind her head. Halley gathered every ounce of fire she had left and willed strength and steadiness to her arm.

She released.

Jared stepped between them, grabbed her wrist before the blow connected, and held her still. "I know how you're feeling right now, but slapping her isn't going to help. She's only doing her job and trust me…you'll only regret the decision later."

"But they broke him. Didn't you hear that? His insides are broken now!" She waved her arms wildly, and her words bordered on hysteria.

"Yes, Halley. I heard everything. But you have two choices at the moment. You can calm down, or I can get out my handcuffs and *make* you calm down."

His golden-eyed stare snuffed out her rage, suffocating the pain like a lid over a candle flame. "But I…"

Jared didn't give her a chance to finish. He slipped his arm behind her knees and lifted her feet off the floor.

She wrapped her arms around his neck and braced against him to ease the bouncing from his heavy steps. His firm, harsh voice vibrated her chest when he hollered back to the paramedics.

"Close this area off, now! Just call the time of death and wait for the detective." He whipped his head in Bo's direction. "Did you get hold of the coroner?"

"Yes. He should be here within the hour."

Halley pushed into Jared. If she got any closer, she might fall right through him. Jared had been in her life since she met Mark, and she'd never seen him act or speak with so much aggression and authority. She'd be lying if she said his mood swings weren't freaking her out. But who could blame him after everything he'd just seen? Maybe subconsciously, she depended on him to be the levelheaded, collected person in the middle of this whirlwind, but that expectation would be unfair and cruel.

Jared glared at Bo and barked a warning. "You and I will discuss this shit show later."

Halley closed her eyes. A tear rolled down her cheek and soaked into the fabric of Jared's shirt just below where her head rested on his chest. She wiped it away, but the floodgates opened, and they flowed freely.

Nothing would ever be the same.

The uncertainty surrounding her life only led to more tears, and heat crept into her cheeks when Jared sidestepped her puke pile. She became aware of the steady rhythm of Jared's heartbeat—predictable and dependable—just like its owner.

The cool wood grazed the back of her bare legs as Jared gently seated her at the table.

Halley tugged the white dress shirt down as far as the length would allow, but without pants, what was the point? If she crossed her legs, maybe she could salvage some dignity.

Jared hunkered down across the refurbished pine table she and Mark had scored at a flea market a few months back.

Halley glided her hand across the smooth wood. "You wanna know something?"

"What's that?"

"I actually tried to talk Mark out of buying this table. Who wouldn't want something like this? The seller had pictures from before they went all DIY. This old thing looked like a piece of crap, but instead of throwing something with potential away, they made a work of art." She shook her head. "And I wanted to pass." Halley looked up. Her eyes were now level with Jared's. "Mark talked them down to $350.00. He always was a good negotiator, but—"

Jared cut her off and pinned her hand down, interrupting the back-and-forth movement and breaking her away from the memory.

"We aren't sitting here to reminisce about the table, Halley. We're sitting here to go over what happened between the last time you saw Mark alive and the time you called for help this morning. So, why don't we start with what you remember about last night."

That was the problem. How was she supposed to tell him what happened last night if she couldn't remember? Everything before the wine was clear, but everything after came in chunks and flashes—a blur of entangled limbs with no recollection of how or why.

Halley released a ragged breath. "I remember coming home from the grocery store around five. Mark was due back from Colorado around six, but his plane had landed early, so he beat me home and surprised me for our anniversary."

Jared freed her hand and plucked a notepad from his pocket. He shook the pen from the spiral binding and clicked the top, exposing the ballpoint tip. "What was Mark doing in Colorado? I don't remember him saying anything to me about a trip to Colorado."

"H-he had to inspect a roller coaster at a new amusement park out there. I guess there was a mechanical issue, so he got called out at the last minute to help."

Halley scratched at the under surface of the table, and tiny slivers of wood buried themselves beneath her nails. Her mind was restless, and her body followed suit, the need to move or even run derailing her train of thought.

Jared blew out a deep breath. "I need you to focus. Is there anything else you can think of? Had he talked to you about anyone giving him a hard time or anything unusual like that?"

"If he had, don't you think I'd have mentioned it? Besides, Mark would've talked to you about something like that before me."

Jared took notes then pinched the bridge of his nose. "Did he bring you a gift for your anniversary? Maybe something out of the ordinary?"

Halley perked up in her chair and flattened her feet against the beige carpet. "Actually, he did. He brought back a bottle of expensive Italian wine."

"Did you drink any?"

"We each had a sip or two…I think. But after that, I can't remember much. I know we danced, and he kissed me." Halley touched her lips. "Then we, well, you know."

Jared waved his arms, signaling silence. "I get the picture. Is there any wine left?"

"Yeah, it's in the fridge." Halley rose from her chair with more control over her legs than she had earlier. Using the counter to steady herself, she strode to the fridge and reached for the towel hanging from the handle to open the door.

"Wait. Don't touch anything," Jared said, nudging her off to the side. "I have gloves on. Try not to handle whatever is in the fridge either. The last thing you want to do is contaminate something the perp might have touched."

She eyed the contents of the fridge. Everything was there—sandwich meat, milk, butter, eggs—everything except the wine. After she shoved the cork back into the neck of the bottle last night, she had tucked it away on the top shelf. She at least remembered that much.

And last time she checked, wine bottles didn't have feet.

Halley could almost feel Jared's eyes burning a hole into the back of her head, so she twisted her neck and peered over her shoulder. "It's not here. I swear on my life, I put the damn thing right there." She pointed to the space where the wine bottle should've been.

"Are you sure that's where you put it?" Jared rubbed his gloved hands together and joined the search.

"Yes, I always put drinks on the top shelf because they stay colder up there."

"Is that really true?"

"Well, the theory has never been proven or anything, but they taste colder to me." She gasped and backed away from the fridge. "Wait! There are two half-full glasses on the coffee table in the living room."

"I had Bo block the area off until the detective assigned to your case arrives," He held up his hands. "You stay here. I'll be right back." Jared sprinted toward the living room. He appeared a few moments later, lips turned down, and his head hung low. "Halley, there are no glasses on the coffee table."

****

Jared searched every inch of the living room for Halley's supposed glasses of wine, to no avail. The detective had arrived at some point during his conversation with Halley, so he needed to be careful not to get in the way or disturb the scene more than he already had. He'd never seen the man before, so the guy must be new.

The detective towered over him by a solid five inches, and the comb-over became evident when he took a step back. Jared attempted to skate out of the living room without being noticed, but the detective hollered over the head of a young man taking pictures.

"Excuse me. Are you Officer Collins?" The detective zigzagged around the gaggle of people who had suddenly filled the room.

"Yes, sir." Jared held out a hand. "What can I do for you?" The man was dressed from neck to ankle in tweed. The weather had begun to cool off as fall rounded the corner, but he had to be sweating his balls off.

The man accepted his outstretched hand and gave a light shake. "I'm Detective Girard Arnold, but you can call me Arnie. Captain Maxwell said you'd be the man to speak with about getting a statement from the victim's wife. Halley, right?"

Jared looked over at his friend.

Mark was surrounded by an entire team of men and women. Some took pictures, while others combed the area for clues or evidence. His body was still displayed across the floor, and within the last thirty minutes, his skin had begun to turn a pale shade of grayish-blue.

When was the damn coroner coming?

"Yes, Arnie. If you can give me a few more minutes, I can get you a statement. She's pretty shaken up, so it's taking a bit longer for her to tell me what happened."

"Have you gotten any information we can use? Did she happen to see the perp? Or do you think she *is* the perp?"

Jared was getting sick and tired of being asked that question. He took one final lingering glance around the room, searching for the elusive glasses, but found nothing. Telling Arnie about the wine and Halley's foggy memory would be the right thing to do—the legal thing, but something wasn't right. He needed more information and concrete evidence. Right now, Halley just sounded like a crazy person grasping at straws. He hated to admit it, but she looked guilty.

"Like I said, she's in shock. She hasn't said much about what happened, but I'm working on getting to the bottom of this. As soon as I finish my report, I'll have the captain sign off and get the file to you ASAP."

One of the women looking over Mark's body yelled Arnie's name.

The detective held up a finger and nodded. "Just do what you can. When you've finished the interview, take her to the precinct. She'll need to be questioned further. Can you manage that?"

Of course he could manage taking her to the precinct—but he didn't want to. Halley was—*is* Mark's wife—and to Jared, that title required a certain standard of loyalty.

He turned and made his way through the archway back to the kitchen where Halley waited. He'd tried his damnedest to be patient, giving her every possible chance to explain herself—to tell him what happened so he could help her, but his efforts were getting him nowhere.

He could spend days on a stakeout or countless hours talking someone down from the ledge, but at this point, his tolerance for games was wearing thin.

Between processing the murder of his best friend and dealing with Halley, Jared couldn't be sure if the glasses had been there when he and Bo arrived.

Halley stopped pacing and stared at him like a deer caught in a pair of headlights.

Jared scratched his head. "Are you sure they were there this morning and you didn't just imagine it?"

Silence hung in the air.

Halley glared at him and planted her fists firmly on her hips. "What exactly are you implying?" He started to speak, but she cut him off. "You think I had something to do with Mark's death, don't you? Do you think I killed my husband?"

"That's not what I said, but even you have to admit…this looks *really* fucking bad." Jared lowered his tone and pressed his face closer to Halley's. "You barely have any memory of last night. You claim there was wine, but we can't find any, and your husband is dead—stabbed at least a dozen times. Yet here you are, not a scratch on you."

Before he could do damage control, they were nose to nose, and he'd gone too far to back down. "Now, unless you can give me something helpful to the investigation, you're gonna have to come down to the station with me and answer more questions for Detective Arnold."

Halley pulled back first and tapped her bare foot against the floor. "You're kidding me, right? You'd really take me to jail because I can't remember any—" She froze, then gasped.

He almost jumped. "What is it? Do you remember something else?"

"Yeah. I can't believe I forgot. Right after I found Mark this morning, I heard the screen door shut." Halley pointed to the door beside them. "When I came out, the big door was wide open. I'm one hundred percent sure I locked up last night, which means someone else had to have been here."

This was getting ridiculous. Calling her a straight-up liar would be rude but come on. Did she honestly expect him to believe someone just snuck in and snuck out after brutally murdering the man she was sleeping beside? Improbable—not impossible—but improbable.

Jared squeezed his eyes shut and pinched the bridge of his nose. The headache brewing behind his temples was bound to be a monster if he didn't take something to relieve the pain soon. Looking at Halley as a friend instead of a suspect only delayed the inevitable. Her story was missing so many pieces he didn't know what to believe. For all he knew, she could just be trying to cover her tracks.

His mind said, *arrest her,* but his gut said, *don't.* And his heart was acting like a defiant teenager and going in a completely different direction—a direction he refused to explore.

None of his internal bashings mattered. As a police officer, he was required to look at the facts, and facing reality meant he needed to take Halley in as a suspect for murder. "Do you have any idea how crazy this all sounds, not to mention implausible?"

Halley stepped back. "Jared, I'm your friend. We've known each other for years. You were the best man at our wedding, for God's sake. You know I wouldn't do this. I couldn't. I know none of this makes any sense, but please, you have to believe me. I *need* you to believe me."

Jared grabbed her hand, pulled her close, and spoke to her like she was a felon, letting his tone go cold. "I have no choice here, Halley. I'm gonna need you to come with me. Obviously, I'm not getting anywhere with you here, so let's not make this any harder than it has to be."

Halley eyed him and made a break for the screen door.

Jared didn't want to take her in like this. But if she wasn't willing to cooperate, then he'd have to get tough. He reached out like lightning and wrapped his hand snugly around her wrist before she could get outside.

Halley squealed, and a sharp pain shot through his chest. This wasn't what he'd signed on for—or maybe it was. How could have guessed that one day he'd be arresting someone he loved?

"Bo!" he hollered as he held Halley's thin wrists behind her back.

Bo peered through the archway and raised a brow at Jared. "Everything all right in here?"

"Everything is fine. I need you to stay here, wait for the coroner, and wrap things up while I take Halley down to the station for questioning. Call Cordini for a ride back. He should be in the area."

"Detective Arnold asked me to swab her hands. They need to test the blood."

"Jesus Christ." This wasn't his first rodeo, but he behaved like this was his first crime scene. He should've taken samples earlier. "Grab the kit and hurry up."

Halley writhed and managed to wriggle loose once more, but she didn't make it any farther than the last time.

Jared tightened his grip and cinched an arm around her waist. The last thing he wanted to do was cuff her, but if she kept struggling, he'd have no other choice.

Bo came back seconds later with a long cotton swab and a tall test tube. "Hold still a second, ma'am. I just need to get some of the blood off your hands."

"Swab them already!"

Bo ran the swab across the palms of Halley's hands and stuck the stick in the tube before adding the small black cap. "Done."

"Great. Now just do what I said, Bo. Okay?"

Bo nodded, and Jared quickly wrangled Halley through the screen door and onto the driveway. Halley repeatedly dropped to her knees, gravel crunched under his boots, and Jared's level of irritability rose by the second.

"Ow! Stop! My feet are hurting." She limped across the small pebbles with her shoeless feet.

Shoes had been the last thing on Jared's mind when he shoved her out the door. The line between officer and friend continued to blur. Bring her in—catch the bad guy—period. But his love for her, and the familiarity of their long-standing friendship, only evoked pangs of guilt and an overwhelming need to protect, not destroy.

Get a grip. Define the line.

Placing his forearm below her ass, he tossed Halley over his shoulder.

Her sobs softened, muffled by her mouth against

his back.

Jared walked back to the house, reached around the door frame to the shoe rack and grabbed the first pair of shoes his hand touched, then went back out.

He laid her gently on the back seat of the squad car, tossed the shoes beside her, slammed the door, then turned his back on everything—the car, Halley, and the crime scene. Air slipped slowly from his lungs as he exhaled, and a sense of calm rolled through his body.

He tapped the hood for luck as he did before and after every call.

He was doing the right thing, wasn't he?

Jared slid into the driver's seat and started the engine. "It's time to go, Halley."

Halley remained silent as he backed out of the driveway.

He took a right at the stop sign and approached the first intersection.

The light turned green immediately.

Maybe the hood tap had worked in his favor. Adjusting his rearview mirror, he caught a glimpse of Halley.

Her eyes widened as she stared out the window.

"What's the—"

There was no time to react, no time to finish his question. A forceful impact sent his squad car careening across four lanes and down an embankment. Glass crackled while groves of trees and a pinwheel of colors surrounded him before the car came to a jarring halt. Everything spun, and the lights outside dimmed. Jared tried to say her name, but his lips wouldn't open. The darkness came slowly, clouding his vision.

Halley…

The darkness smothered him.

****

Bo glared at Mark's body. Seeing the man who ruined his life—dead as a doornail—twisted his emotions in a way he couldn't quite grasp. Should he be happy? Should he feel some sense of satisfaction that justice had been served? An entire year of planning, over in the blink of a stab wound.

He adjusted the rubber gloves at his wrist and folded the blanket Mark had been lying on, then inserted it into a large, clear, plastic bag. He zipped the bag closed and studied the blanket's pattern—black-and-yellow swirls brought together by oversized white daisies. Well, they used to be white.

"Here's the blanket, Detective. Bagged and tagged."

Arnie took the evidence and placed the bag into a clear tote beside the couch. "Thank you, Officer Frazer."

"You're welcome." Bo shifted his stance. "So, do you have any ideas about what might've happened here?"

Arnie scoffed. "I've been investigating homicides for the better part of three decades, and some of them have been downright gruesome. This one, though..." He trailed off for a moment. "This one was pure vengeance. The first two stab wounds would've easily killed the man, but whoever did this stabbed him fifteen times, by my count."

"Do you think the wife could be guilty?"

Arnie shrugged. "Too soon to tell, but as of right now, she's our number-one suspect. Hell, she's our only suspect, at least until we can find evidence to prove otherwise. We haven't found the murder weapon, and there was no indication that someone broke in. Hopefully, Officer Collins was able to get a telling statement from her." He motioned to the paramedic struggling to get the body onto the stretcher. "Why don't you go help her?" He pulled a card from his shirt pocket. "When you see Officer Collins later, could you tell him to give me a call?"

"Sure thing, Detective." Bo strolled over to the fireplace and grabbed the bottom of the body bag from the cute brunette paramedic Halley almost decked earlier. "Here, this is heavy. Let me help you."

The male paramedic had vanished, so he activated the stretcher's brakes before helping the young woman hoist the bag off the ground.

The coroner, Steve, had come and gone in a flash. Apparently, Mark wasn't the only person who kicked the bucket today, and he didn't have room to transport another body.

"Thanks." She scrunched up her nose. "My name is Kyra, by the way."

After lowering Mark's stiff body onto the stretcher, he reached out. "Bo. Bo Frazer."

"It's nice to meet you, Bo." Kyra nodded at the black bag and tugged her high ponytail tight against the top of her head. "Quite a bloodbath here today, wasn't it? Did you know the victim?"

Bo shook his head. He couldn't tell her he'd spent the last seven years wishing for a reckoning—for the day Mark Martin got what he deserved. Only, this wasn't quite what he had in mind. Seems he wasn't the only one who had a bone to pick with that asshole. "No, I didn't know him, but he was my partner's best friend." The hairs on the back of his neck stood as the words slipped out. Damn. He shouldn't have said that.

When he moved to Charlotte, Bo had a plan…a simple and straightforward plan. Get close to the target and take him down. Then his years of suffering would be over, and justice would be served.

Only someone seemed to have taken the *down* part literally.

He hadn't figured on fitting in or enjoying life in Charlotte. But Jared took him under his wing like a brother. If Jared ever found out what Bo had done, his partner would never speak to him again.

"Hey, Bo?"

Bo's head snapped up. "Hmm?"

"Did you hear what I said?"

Rambling thoughts distracted him. His pants could've been on fire, and he wouldn't have noticed. "No, I'm sorry. I didn't."

"I just asked if you'd like to go out for drinks one night this week." Kyra wrote her number on a gum wrapper and handed it to Bo. "Give me a call when you decide."

He stared at the number for a moment and waved her away. "Will do."

Kyra and the other paramedic, who had suddenly reemerged, wheeled the stretcher out through the front door.

Bo waited until they were out of sight to survey the scene at his own pace. He looked around. All accusations rested on Halley, but Bo didn't buy them. And given his partner's snippy attitude earlier, clearly, Jared didn't either. There was more to this murder than anyone knew.

He walked out the back and opened his phone. "Hi, Steve, it's Officer Frazer."

Steve Boullard had held his position as county coroner for the past thirty-five years. He wore excessive cologne to cover up the bourbon scent and had less hair than an infant. After his wife left him for a dentist last year, drinking became his second profession, along with frequenting the local strip joint. Rumors swarmed around the precinct. Steve was on his way out. His new bride wanted a change of scenery, and the man wasn't the type to say no.

Bo needed to take advantage while he still had the chance.

"Didn't I just see you?"

Bo snickered. "Yeah, sorry. I wondered if you wouldn't mind doing a tox screen for me after you receive the body."

"Is there any particular reason for me to perform a tox screen? You know I'm not supposed to do that without a good reason and an order from Captain Maxwell."

"The suspect was rambling on about wine. She swears there was some at the scene earlier, but we can't seem to find any. I need to make sure we check all the boxes in this investigation. So, what do ya say?"

Steve sighed. "Sure. I should have the results back by tomorrow afternoon."

"Thanks, Steve. I owe ya." Bo stopped for a moment. "Oh, and Steve?"

"Yeah?"

"Let's keep this between us."

Steve sighed. "Is this going to get me fired? What exactly are you up to?"

"This isn't for me. I need to know for Jared."

"Jared? What's he got to do with this case?"

"Don't ask any more questions, okay? The less you know, the better." Bo peeled his gloves off and clenched his hands. "Can you do the screening or not?"

"Fine, but only because Jared is a damn good cop…and friend. He stopped me from getting a DUI when my wife left me last year, and I owe him big time. But if Captain Maxwell finds out about this, I'm blaming everything on you. Got it?"

"I'll take full responsibility, Steve. Thanks again."

Chapter Three

Halley braced herself for impact. The oversized oak tree was closer and closer with every passing second, and the cage used for dividing the good guys from the bad ones gave her something to hold onto.

The accident happened so fast. The rusty blue pickup didn't bother to brake at the red light.

Halley wanted to warn Jared, but by the time her mouth caught up with her brain, they'd been hit.

What were the odds of two heinous things happening to her in less than twenty-four hours? Questioning her luck was a waste of time because clearly, it was better than she ever could have guessed.

Maybe the universe wanted her gone. Perhaps this was God's way of saying, "*Sorry, Halley, but your time is up.*" After all, being involved in two car accidents over twenty years was a bit much. And the first one stole both her parents. Sometimes, on the bad days, she wished that crash had taken her too.

Halley gripped the diamond-shaped wire barrier, and a sharp pain sliced through her wrist as the car hit the tree with a *smash*. Tiny shards of glass slapped her face and embedded into her hair and skin. Her time wasn't up quite yet apparently.

She had to look up, but part of her didn't want to. Jared could be dead, and regardless of his stance on her innocence, he was her only viable lifeline—her final connection to Mark and the life she once knew. If he didn't survive the crash, then she had no one.

Her head throbbed, and twinges of pain crawled up her neck when she lifted her head. She climbed onto the back seat and crushed her face against the divider.

Jared's back rose and fell.

Thank God. His breaths seemed steady, but his head was slumped against the steering wheel, and a thin trail of blood traveled from his ear to his cheek.

Halley twisted her stiff neck to the left. *Damn whiplash.* The thick brush reduced her view of the landscape, allowing only a small glimpse of the babbling stream below. Someone would come to rescue them before long, and her gratitude was quickly replaced by a racing heart and shaking hands.

They wouldn't waste any time packing her up and taking her straight to jail. Without a plan, she'd spend the rest of her life utilizing stainless-steel toilets and peeing with an audience—at least that's how it went in the movies. She'd never actually talked to anyone in the county jail, let alone a maximum-security prison, which was probably where she'd go.

Halley shook off the chill that passed through her half-naked body and eyed the broken window beside her. The glass arced in a bunch of thin lines like fireworks on the Fourth of July. She reached for the door handle and tugged. Nothing.

Crap.

Silly woman, you can't open back doors from inside the cop car.

Time to be resourceful.

Halley scoured the back for something—anything she could use to get the hell out of the car. She reached under Jared's seat and retrieved one of her flip-flops. Ugh. Only a man would grab the two foam pieces and completely ignore the hiking boots sitting right beside them, but whatever. Beggars couldn't be choosers. But where was the other one? After searching under both seats, Halley came up empty-handed. She dove her hand into the seat's crack and yelped when she yanked out the lost flip-flop.

At least one thing went her way today.

She slipped on her shoes and rested her back against the seat, placing both feet flat against the window. She pulled her knees back and thrust them forward. The glass cracked and crinkled like she was stepping on thin ice. Again, she kicked the window until finally, it gave way under pressure.

Halley stuck her arm outside and lifted the door handle, wincing as the cool metal touched one of her many cuts. The door refused to budge, so she slammed her shoulder against the side panel until she ran out of breath. Ridiculous. The crash had most likely damaged the hinges. She was wasting time. One final option remained—she'd have to crawl out.

Careful not to cut her knees on the stragglers of glass stuck in the window, Halley stood and leaned outside. She wrapped her arm around a low-hanging branch and strained—*ouch*! A jagged piece of glass caught her outer thigh. The wound didn't look too deep, but she couldn't maneuver into a position close enough to inspect the cut. Halley brought up her other leg, groaning as sharp edges nicked her fragile flesh. Her body dangled from the branch until she released her hands and hit the ground knees down, ass up.

She crawled to the driver's-side door and yanked

on the handle.

Jared's door was jammed too, so she rapped on the window. "Jared? Are you okay?" She knocked one more time. "I don't know if you can hear me, but I have to go. I'm so sorry. You may not believe me now, but I swear I'm innocent. And I'm going to prove it."

A muffled groan pierced through the thick glass, but Jared's body remained still.

Hell would have to freeze over before she'd willingly go to jail for a murder she didn't commit.

Halley surveyed the area, or what she could see, anyway. It didn't take long to figure out her location. She'd explored these trails and terrain a million times in the last decade. Hiking was the only thing that kept her from going stir-crazy when Mark left for work. He could be gone for weeks. Hell, one time, he got held up on a build in Texas, and she didn't see him for three months.

"Hey, lady!" A pudgy man waving a cell phone in the air yelled down to her. "I called the police. Are you okay? I swear I tried to stop!"

Yeah, right.

Halley said nothing to the man. Instead, she moved through the brush and followed the stream.

Twenty miles west, deep in Charlotte, Pennsylvania's rugged mountain wilderness, stood an off-the-grid cabin utterly isolated from the outside world and off anyone's radar.

Ever the doomsday theorist, Mark insisted the cabin be completely self-sustainable. They spent countless hours building, driving nails, and stocking the pantry shelves with canned food and toiletries. He'd paid for everything in cash and warned her to tell no one of their activities…not even Jared.

How Mark obtained the land was still murky at best. Honestly, she was reasonably concerned over the legality, and he never produced a deed, but then again, he never offered Halley details on much of anything. As Mark's dutiful housewife, finances and investments weren't her concern, so she never bothered to question him about goings-on that didn't involve cooking, cleaning, or laundry.

Nevertheless, the cabin would allow her the sanctuary of seclusion until she could figure this all out.

Halley's arm hung limp, and the swelling snuck up with a vengeance. Waves of nausea roiled in her gut, thanks to the constant throbbing—like a toothache pulsing through her whole body. She wasn't exactly in the right frame of mind or the proper attire, but if she didn't leave now, it'd be game over.

She peered over her shoulder at Jared one last time and planted her feet squarely against the stream's edge.

The moon would be centered in the sky when she reached the cabin.

Her body revolted against the thought.

Halley had never been a fan of the night. Not because of the darkness, but because she couldn't see what was hiding within the veil. Monsters lurked in the shadows, and if she couldn't see them, then how was she supposed to fight?

What kind of monsters would be waiting for her when she wandered into the forest? This was their world, and she didn't belong.

Sirens wailed in the distance, and regardless of readiness, there was only one thing left to do. Run.

****

She couldn't help but giggle when Jared dragged Halley from the house. The melodramatic, excessive show Halley put on was quite a sight to behold, as she bounced around and fell to the ground like a toddler not getting their way in the supermarket.

Ridiculous.

A tender tune floated through the air from inside her purse, growing louder as she dug to the bottom. She moved the oversized wallet her mother had given her last Christmas and retrieved her brand-new phone.

The phone was slim and sleek, with a red back and a tempered-glass screen protector.

Mark had begged her to keep their secret—paid a nice chunk of money too.

No way could she afford a phone this nice otherwise.

If Mark had stuck to the plan and kept his promises, he wouldn't have had to pay with his life.

Men. They never learned.

She brought the phone to her ear and groaned. "What's the matter? I told you not to call me unless there was an emergency."

The male voice on the other end was squeaky and childish, like nails on a chalkboard, only worse. "W-well, I just wanted to make sure you got out of the house all right."

"For the love of God. Don't you think if something had gone wrong, you would've known by now?" He was the last person on earth she'd wanted to get tangled up with, but the man was stupid, gullible, naïve, and desperate—all the things she needed in an accomplice. He'd follow her blindly until he served his purpose. After that, she'd just get rid of him and start anew far away from the shit show that had somehow become her life.

He cleared his throat and whispered, "I know. I'm sorry. It's just that…" he paused. "I worry about you. You know I love you, right?"

Gross.

His love was genuine and sent her gag reflex into overtime. Unfortunately, his presence had become a necessity, at least for the time being. It seemed in her best interest to play along. "I'm aware. And I, uh, love you too." She stuck out her tongue then covered her mouth to stop her lunch from making an untimely exit.

"I'm so glad you feel the same way," he said.

"Sure…me too. Listen, I'm going now. Don't call me again. If I need anything, I'll call you." She tucked the phone back into her purse and allowed her body one quick shiver of disgust before moving on with her day. There was so much work to be done in such a small window of time.

She didn't have a minute to lose.

****

The white light burned his eyes like someone threw sand in them. Did he die?

"Where am I?" His gravelly voice surprised him. He'd smoked one cigarette his entire life yet sounded as if he sucked down a pack a day.

"Hey, hey, buddy. You're on the third floor at the hospital. Lie still a minute, okay? I'll go get someone."

"Wait." Jared couldn't quite put a face to the blurry person on the other side of the room, but his voice held the key. "Bo?" He rubbed his eyes, but that only made them throb more. "Is that you?"

"Yeah, it's me. Do you need anything? Water,

beer, or maybe a hooker?"

Jared laughed then instantly regretted it. He groaned as the pain around his ribcage intensified. "Can you come closer? I can't see a damn thing."

As Bo came closer, Jared's vision cleared. "That's better. Now, what the hell happened? I remember bits and pieces, but…" Snapshots of trees and spinning flitted into his consciousness before fizzling out again. If he was in a hospital bed, then something really fucking bad must've happened.

He lifted his head off the pillow. Everything in the room spun, including Bo. He shut his eyes tight and let his head fall back against the not-so-soft rock hospitals always tried to pass off as a pillow. If he moved his head too much, there might be the consequence of an upchuck.

"Whoa. Take it easy and hand me that big remote-looking thing beside you."

"Why? Are we going to watch television?" Jared felt around. "Just please don't put on any of those ridiculous reality shows you like. I can't handle watching any more catfights." If this was what being blind was like, he wanted no part of it—being helpless was way beyond his comfort zone.

Tightening his fingers around the oversized block, he held it in the air.

Bo snatched the remote without missing a beat.

Jared heard the click of a button followed by a soft beep.

"There," Bo said. "It's not a remote for the TV, and a nurse or someone should be in any minute."

"That's all fine and dandy, but you still didn't answer my question." Jared cracked his eyes open, slower this time, which helped them adjust to the harsh lights.

"Well, uh, you were in a pretty nasty accident. I came on the scene just as the call came in. When I got out and saw your squad car at the bottom, I thought…" Bo ran a hand through his hair. "Honestly, you're lucky to be alive. Don't you remember?"

"Lucky? I can tell you with complete certainty that my ribs don't feel like they hit the jackpot by any means. And no, I don't remember much about the accident at all." Jared closed his eyes and inhaled deeply. The overpowering sting of antiseptic choked him, and his dry throat burned. His eyes brimmed with tears, and he crossed his arms around his rib cage, hugging himself tight. His attempt to chase the pain away and keep his chest and stomach from moving was in vain.

"Yeah, I hear broken ribs can be pretty painful."

"Jesus. How many broke? All of them?" Jared rolled, but the excruciating pain kicked him back.

Bo pulled the hospital mug off the small wooden tray beside the bed and put the straw to Jared's lips.

Jared wrapped his lips around the straw and sucked in. The ice-cold liquid extinguished most of the fire, leaving a manageable smolder, returning his mouth to a wet oasis instead of a sticky glue trap.

The other man shrugged. "They wouldn't give me any information, but I heard the doc and his nurse talking in the hallway. I think he said you broke two ribs and have a minor concussion, but don't quote me on that."

Jared licked his lips and pushed the up arrow on the clunky bedside remote. The bed rose, and his back stretched in a hallelujah sort of way. "Why wouldn't they tell you anything?"

"I'm not your emergency contact."

The entire incident flooded back, and the strange feeling from earlier slammed into him like a bullet against Kevlar. Mark and Captain Maxwell were Jared's emergency contacts. He had nobody else—and now he was minus one more.

His eyes widened, and his fingers trembled around the bed rail. Mark's death, arresting Halley, and the accident.

It was all there—every horrifying moment.

The look on Bo's face did nothing to calm his fears.

Bo set the cup on the table and hit the call button again. "Settle down. Everything is gonna be fine. Nurse!" he yelled from the bedside.

"I don't know what's happening to me. Why can't I stop shaking, and where is Halley?"

"Jared. You need to chill. When they pulled you out, Halley wasn't in the car. We combed the entire area, and she was nowhere to be found. Captain Maxwell thinks she took off."

That slowed his heart rate down slightly, but he couldn't get the shaking under control. "I'm sorry, I don't know why I can't stop shaking. Damn. Even my teeth are chattering."

"Panic attacks will do that to you." The soft, confident voice came from the doorway.

A panic attack? Who would've thought? Jared had heard about them during a presentation at work but always assumed the people experiencing them were overreacting. He was wrong.

"Officer Frazer, I need you to leave the room for a few minutes, please. I'll call you back in when we're finished." The petite nurse in forest-green scrubs stopped at Jared's side. Her long curly hair was tied back in a half-assed ponytail. And when the sun hit, the locks lit up like fire.

"It's good to see you, Mags." Jared tried to smile.

Maggie Walker grew up with Mark and Jared on Pickler Street. Jared always said he and Mark were the fire while she was the extinguisher. She took care of them, kept them out of any trouble that could land them behind bars, and forced them to be somewhat civilized, all while being the most sought-after girl at Grantley High.

She'd recently relocated to her parents' house due to a nasty divorce. Her asshat ex-husband, Trent, left her with nothing but a garbage bag full of clothes and ten thousand dollars in credit-card debt.

Scumbag.

Maggie checked his IV and fiddled with the machine that held a bag of who knew what. She handed him two pills and kissed him on the cheek. "Take a deep breath and swallow both those pills. They'll aid in managing the pain and help you rein in the panic." She wrote something on his chart and hooked it back onto the foot of the bed. "I'm happy to see you're awake and talking like you didn't just fly down an embankment and live."

"What hit us, a tour bus?"

Maggie shook her head. "From what I gathered, it was less of a bus and more like a full-sized pickup."

Jared lowered his head and grasped Maggie's long slender fingers. "Did you hear about Mark?"

41

She didn't have to say a word. The way her head dropped at the sound of his name said all he needed to know.

"Yes. I heard." She blew out a deep breath. "Although I still don't think the news has sunk in. I can't believe he's really gone."

"I know what you mean," he whispered. "I don't understand how this could've happened. I don't know how Halley could've—"

Maggie raised her hand to silence him. "Are you being serious right now? You don't honestly believe Halley is responsible for Mark's death, do you?" Her emerald eyes were wild and furious and filled with pain. "You and I both know how much she loved him. How much they loved each other."

He did. He'd been a part of their entire relationship, from beginning...to end. He even delivered the most-epic best-man speech of all time after four tequila bombers and half a bottle of champagne. A mistake neither Mark nor Halley ever let him live down. "You didn't see it, Mags. You don't know how it looked, so don't tell me what I should and shouldn't believe. Besides, Mark didn't just die." Jared lowered his voice. "He was murdered. And I don't want her to be involved any more than you do."

"Murdered?" Maggie slumped onto the edge of the bed. "I-I can't believe...I mean, I'd heard about his passing, but nobody told me how he died." She fiddled with the silver ring on her middle finger. "You're right, though. I didn't see what you saw. But in my heart, I know Halley is innocent, and of all the people who should be fighting for her, it seems like you've basically given up."

"Mags, come on, don't be like that."

"I'm not *being* like anything, Jared. But I do think you're jumping to conclusions, and maybe you should have a little faith."

All the evidence pointed in Halley's direction, even if he didn't want to see or believe what was right in front of him. On the other hand, Maggie did have a point. Maybe he was jumping to conclusions. He desperately wanted to hold someone—anyone—accountable for Mark's death. Who wouldn't? Regardless, a piece of him blamed her.

"So, you don't think she's the killer?"

"No, I honestly don't." Maggie patted his hand and kissed his cheek again. "I'm not going to tell you what to do, because you aren't going to listen to me anyway. But can you promise me one thing?"

"Possibly." He shrugged and winced. "Depends on what I'm promising."

"That if you find her before the cops do, you'll hear her out."

"All right." He rested his head back against the rock-hard pillow. "I promise. But don't think for one minute that I won't toss her in a jail cell to rot if she can't provide some solid proof of her innocence."

"Understood. Just lie still for a few minutes. The doctor will be in to check you over, and if all your tests come back normal, he'll discharge you in a couple of hours." Maggie half-heartedly smiled and headed toward the door, leaving it slightly ajar when she left.

Bo poked his head inside, and Jared motioned for him to enter.

Bo cleared his throat. "Jared, I want to apologize for what happened at the crime scene earlier. You know, with the paramedics and everything."

He'd almost forgotten about that, but there was no point in dredging up old mistakes. He never enjoyed living in the past anyway. "I'm sorry too. I got kinda carried away with all the chaos. You did what you thought was right. No harm, no foul." Jared cleared his throat. "I'm gonna need a ride when I'm done here, though."

"Sure. Not a problem. You just need me to drive you home?"

"Uh, no."

Bo scratched the back of his neck, then lifted a can of pop from the tray and cracked the aluminum tab. "Okay. If I'm not taking you home, then where are we going?"

"Back to the crime scene."

Chapter Four

Night fell fast as she entered the deepest thickets of the forest. The full moon lit the winding trails, and stars shimmered in the cloudless sky above. Owls hunted with warning hoots, and coyotes voiced about their latest kill.

A bat dive-bombed her from a tree limb above, and she ducked.

She'd be lying if she said walking alone in the forest at night wasn't downright terrifying. She'd also be lying if she said the thought of turning back hadn't crossed her mind. Spending the rest of her life in prison would suck, but getting eaten alive ranked high on her list of shitty things that could happen but probably wouldn't.

In one of her outdoor magazines, Halley had read that animals could smell fear. Her body throbbed. She leaned against the rough trunk of the wide maple that stood steady and solid to her right and steadied her breathing. *In and out, in and out.*

She tilted her head back and counted the stars until she was calm enough to continue. The chill of fall cut right through her sweat, and if she stopped for too long, she'd freeze. Her feet had been bleeding for hours, leaving trickles of blood on the crunchy leaves.

Flip-flops were great for a casual stroll down Main Street, but hell for hiking.

A low grumble reverberated off the trees, echoing through the vast forest.

Halley crouched down at the base of the tree and scanned the area. The moon lit the landscape just enough to make out simple shapes and landmarks around her.

The growl sounded again before a soul-crushing howl echoed through the air...closer this time.

A pair of glowing eyes, white as snow when ignited by the full moon, peered between two thin trees on her left. She couldn't see what kind of animal was staring her down, but her window of opportunity to escape was shrinking.

Limbs cracked as it slyly and slowly gained ground.

She was being hunted.

Between her blood trail and the noise she made, she assumed the animal had probably been tracking her for a while. She was injured and weak—the perfect opportunity for an easy meal for her stalker.

Halley's head snapped up, and she studied the trail ahead, calculating the distance in her mind.

She looked down at the rocks surrounding the tree to her right. Speckles of green glow in dark paint caught her eye.

Mark had tried to make the markers inconspicuous by having them only visible at night.

She was almost there—three minutes, tops. As soon as she crested the hill, she'd have a clear view of the cabin and a refuge from the harsh, unforgiving nature that surrounded her.

The animal stepped out of the shadows and limped toward her. With every step, the beast released an ear-piercing screech.

Whatever wanted to eat her was also injured. This gave her an edge she didn't have before and one she intended to take full advantage of.

Moonlight illuminated the sleek fur and pointed ears.

Halley could barely make out the snout cast in shadows, but when its lips retracted, jagged teeth glistened.

A coyote.

Her stalker was a fucking coyote.

Irony had a sense of humor after all. Last year, Mark and Jared had taken her coyote hunting, and they both got one apiece while she ate pretzels and drank pop until the button on her jeans almost burst. The predator had now become the prey, and she'd fallen a notch on the food chain. Judging by his emaciated appearance, the bastard was hungry—starving actually, possibly rabid, and his howl echoed his intent to kill.

Coyotes weren't usually considered large enough to take down a human, but he was bigger than any she'd seen before—easily the size of a large dog. Given her spot on death's doorstep, his desperation for a warm-blooded meal, and his four legs against her two, the odds were in his favor.

Her core went cold.

Halley kicked off her flip-flops and brushed them to the side. There was no way she could outrun anything in those shoes. Today had ignited a desire to live—to survive—revealing an internal will she'd believed had died with her parents. Life had more to offer. Thirty was young, and Mark would want her to keep going. He'd want her to fight. She dug her feet into the dirt, just like when she ran for the high school track team. She set the tips of her fingers in place and lifted her ass to the sky.

Ready. Set. Go.

Halley bolted, the sound of a gun reverberating in the distance. Weird. Hunting after dark was illegal. She tucked in her elbows and pushed harder. Maybe she'd imagined the blast. Stress-induced hallucinations were real. They'd plagued her once before.

No. Now wasn't the time. She needed to run.

Her feet pounded against the ground in a rhythmic stride. Branches stabbed her feet, and the leaves were slick from last night's rain.

Rustling and snarling echoed through the air, dominating the quiet forest.

If she looked back, he'd have her.

She kept her eyes on the markers and focused on her breathing. The tin cabin roof caught her attention as the moonlight bounced off its ridges. She was so close she could taste the victory. Her foot connected with the first step, and she dove for the welcome mat, tossing the rubber rectangle to the side. She fumbled for the key resting flat against the wood and grunted when the cold metal slipped through her fingers.

The coyote whimpered, but she was fresh out of fucks as to why. She snatched the key off the porch and scrambled to her feet, sliding the metal into the lock. When the lock clicked, she twisted the doorknob and sighed as it opened instantly, the threshold welcoming her without resistance.

Nails *clacked* as the coyote reached the porch, so she twirled like a ballerina and slammed the door. Given the muffled *yelp*, she assumed she had hit him in the snout.

Served him right.

She heaved her exhausted body onto the pine floor and let her overheated skin cool itself on the chilled wood. Her fingers grazed every inch of skin. Was she missing any limbs? No. All body parts were still intact and accounted for. The gash on her leg burned, and she winced as her hand passed over the wound. But she'd assess the aches, pains, and damages later. She'd made it, and that's what mattered.

Her stomach ached from lack of water and food, but she had nothing left.

Rolling her head in an awkward circle, Halley inspected her surroundings.

Almost a year had passed since the last time she stepped foot inside the cabin. Mark often came up to check on the building and stock the cupboards, but she was never interested in tagging along…and if memory served, he never asked.

Vacancy left visible marks on the inside. Sheets protected the furniture, and dust violated the floorboards while intricately detailed cobwebs shimmered, stretched across the corners. A stream of moonlight dusted the floor and revealed the outline of a footprint near her right hand.

Mark hadn't been up here for the better part of six months—at least not to her knowledge.

She raised her arm as high as it would allow, but the swelling weighed down the limb. Her arm dropped with a thud, and searing pain traveled from her wrist to her shoulder. A shrill bellow passed through her lips, followed by the wave of nausea she'd grown disturbingly accustomed to. When she turned her head back to the footprint, most of the sole's design had been distorted by the fanning motion of her arm.

Damn. Tomorrow Halley would get her shit together. She'd splint her arm, get some water from the creek down below, and figure out how to deal with her utterly screwed-up circumstances.

She tucked her knees underneath the once-white dress shirt for warmth. There was a queen-sized bed in the other room but moving wasn't an option. She cleansed her lungs and quieted her mind, too tired to keep track of her racing thoughts. Unconsciousness took control without a fight, lulling her into a land where reality could be paused…if only for a moment.

****

A couple of broken ribs, a cut above his eyebrow, and approximately one hundred bruises ganged up on him as he gingerly climbed into the passenger side of Bo's rugged old pickup.

The moon had replaced the sun, and the stars glimmered in the clear night sky.

"Aren't you going to buckle up?" Bo jeered.

"Hardy-har-har. Anyone ever tell you that you're funnier after you've punched out for the night?"

"Actually, no. But thanks for noticing." Bo tapped the steering wheel. "You know, you could lose your badge for going back into the crime scene without permission. And I could lose mine too, if anyone found out I helped you be a dumbass."

"I swear on my life, no one will ever know you did this. I'd give up my badge willingly before ever screwing over my partner."

Bo grinned. "I appreciate that."

They'd only been partners for six months.

Bo had transferred from Blackstone, a small town similar to Charlotte, a few hours away. He rarely overshared, and Jared never asked, so naturally they worked well together. His attendance wasn't an issue, he had Jared's back, and his peculiar sense of humor helped lighten the mood when things got tough.

Jared *usually* played by the rules, never leaving any stone unturned. If Bo stepped out of line, Jared was quick to nudge him back in. Maybe that was why Captain Maxwell paired them together.

Oddly enough, Jared had been straddling the line separating right and wrong since this morning.

His phone vibrated against his leg. *Speak of the devil.* "Captain. What can I do for you?

"Collins. Where are you?"

Jared turned his head to look at his partner, whose stare never strayed from the road. "I'm on my way home. Bo's giving me a ride." How much information should he dish out? Whatever. He was bound to find out sooner or later. "I, uh, was in a car accident earlier, and the hospital just released me."

"Do you think I'm an idiot, Collins? They called me the minute you were admitted, and they also said they were trying to reach a Mark Martin regarding your admittance. Would that be the same Mark Martin who was murdered earlier this morning?"

Damned emergency contact form.

"Yes, sir, it is, but listen—"

"No, Collins. You listen. You're one of my best officers, but you gave me no indication that you had personal involvement with the Martins when I spoke with you this morning. That is a blatant disregard for the protocol, and I will not allow a conflict of interest to screw with this investigation. Detective Arnold is already after my hide because I never received your report with the wife's statement."

Crap. Halley's statement had to be in the car somewhere, if anything was left of the old clunker. Having her ramblings disappear would be even better. He did his job. He took her statement and had every intention of turning it in. And the accident wasn't his fault, which meant nobody could blame him for the missing paperwork. "I'm sorry, sir, but—"

"Save your breath. Now we have a suspect on the run and no leads as to her whereabouts. I hate to do this, but pending further investigation into the matter, you are temporarily suspended."

Jared ran his hand down his face, even though a suspension was probably for the best. Honestly, he'd planned on taking a leave of absence so he could delve into Mark's death without Detective Arnold and the captain breathing down his neck. This wasn't a case he could just relinquish to someone else, and he owed it to Mark to catch his killer. "So, who will be taking over the case?"

"Cordini and Frazer. And I don't want to hear another word about any of this. Stay home, heal up, and keep your damn nose out of this case. Do you understand?"

Bo taking on the case, Jared could deal with, but Cordini was a whiny, manipulative mama's boy. Thirty-five, still living at home in his mom's basement, and the man didn't even know the difference between a misdemeanor and a felony. Everybody on the force knew Stan Cordini's uncle, Clarence Cordini, the mayor of Charlotte, got the slacker the job. Cordini definitely wasn't hired for his skills.

"Yes, sir. Oh, one more thing. Did Lily get into that expensive college she applied to?"

"This conversation is over, Collins."

That was a yes.

"Don't do anything stupid." Captain Maxwell ended the call with a loaded warning.

But the likelihood of follow-through was slim—scratch that—none.

Jared slid the phone into his shirt pocket and flicked his partner's arm. "Did you know I would be suspended? And that Cordini would replace me on the case?"

Bo's Adam's apple jumped when he swallowed. "Yeah, I knew. Captain Maxwell called me while you were getting your final round of tests done. I wanted to tell you, but he said I'd be suspended too if I said anything."

"It's all right, I understand. I mean, don't get me wrong, I'm beyond pissed, but I understand."

"Thanks, Jared." Bo turned the wheel and whipped his truck into Mark and Halley's driveway. "Here we are. And listen, I promise not to let Cordini jack up the investigation. We *will* figure out what happened to your friend."

Jared swore his heart skipped a beat at the word *friend*. Mark was so much more than that. Captain Maxwell could climb a rope for all he cared—this investigation belonged to Jared, and he intended to break the case wide open.

His ribs throbbed like someone had been banging on them with a mallet as he slowly pried himself out of the truck. He clutched the door handle and paused.

"Just let him think he's part of the investigation, but don't let that idiot be responsible for anything important. Lord knows, he'll mess up. Cordini fucks up everything he touches…which is why Captain Maxwell always puts him on coffee duty."

Jared slammed the rusty truck door, and Bo nodded through the glass. They shared an understanding he was grateful for. What the captain didn't know wouldn't hurt him.

When Bo's taillights disappeared, Jared started toward the back door, stopping just short of the porch steps.

A muffled rustling emanated from inside.

Just like when he arrived that morning, the big wooden door hung wide open, but the screen door was latched.

An animal could've easily wandered in had someone neglected to shut the door on their way out. But judging by the torn, hanging caution tape, that wasn't going to be the case.

Jared lifted the bottom of his T-shirt, wrapped his cloaked fingers around the handle, and pulled down, waiting for the *click*.

The shuffling ceased immediately.

He snatched the flashlight from his belt and shone the bright beam around the empty kitchen, the stale scent of blood once again infiltrating his nostrils.

Jared stepped inside, bringing the flashlight level to his chin. As he turned to face the living room, a blur of black rushed him, tossing a shoulder right into his ribs. He fell back, the air expelled abruptly from his lungs, and the black blob scrambled to their feet.

No fucking way were they going to get off that

easy. For all he knew, they could be solely responsible for Mark's death, and they could clear Halley's name. But what if Halley was the one under the mask? His mind raced, but he had to shut down his thoughts. He needed to be quick.

Jared grabbed an ankle and jammed his elbow into the back of his assailant's kneecap.

They fell hard, and a loud *thwap* rang out before the figure broke free and ran, flinging the screen door open.

Jared rolled to his side and hoisted himself up, using the towel hanging from the fridge. Attempting to run after whoever was hidden under the night-colored clothes and ski mask was pointless.

Damn.

He'd missed his chance. They'd be long gone before his feet touched the grass. He grunted. He might not have caught them, but they'd have one hell of a sore leg tomorrow. A 9-1-1 call would be in order, but, if Captain Maxwell or the detective found out Jared was snooping around a crime scene without permission, not to mention while under suspension, his badge would disappear like beer during happy hour. The rules needed to be bent—okay, obliterated—for a little longer.

Jared's flashlight shone from beneath the old grandfather clock. He slid his hand underneath and, with more effort than he cared to admit, he hooked his finger around the handle and pulled it to him.

The cherry-red clock had been in Mark's family for generations. Would Halley keep the archaic timepiece?

He reached up and winced, running a finger along the minute hand. Even when they were kids, the clock couldn't keep the right time. Now would be as good a time as any to look at the mechanics up close. Hell, maybe he could even fix the clunky thing.

He opened the door, and the pendulum swayed slowly—back and forth. Most grandfather clocks showed off the swinging brass through a glass door, but this one was different. The door was opaque and cut from the deepest red wood he'd ever seen. The gentle motion of the clock's insides soothed his churning stomach. He aimed the flashlight at the lowest section of the clock and crouched.

Why was the small board off-kilter and tilted? He tugged on a pair of gloves he kept on hand for emergencies, grabbed the survival knife from his pocket, and slid the blade under the board, prying it just high enough so he could get his fingers around the edge. The cockeyed piece of wood lifted with ease.

"I'll be damned." He set the wood down. "A false bottom."

A manilla envelope weighted down by a cheap-looking flip phone shone in the light.

Jared lifted the phone and studied the scuffed plastic. Did they even make phones like this anymore? This must be what the intruder was after.

He stuck the flashlight in between his teeth and pinched the metal tabs on the envelope together. The flap lifted, and his instincts begged him to call Detective Arnold—to fulfill his duty as a man of the law. But the rogue part he so often suppressed beckoned him to look inside. What could be so important that someone would go through this much trouble to get it out of the house?

Jared dipped his fingers into the envelope and

Secluded

pulled out a stack of pictures. Pictures of Mark and, from what he counted, at least a dozen different women. Women who weren't Halley.

"Jesus, Mark, what did you do?" he whispered.

The final photo in the stack wasn't a photo at all. Bringing the paper closer to his face, Jared studied it. Different-colored lines and drawings filled the sheet, and X marked a spot. A map.

Mark's shady involvement in some serious shit went far beyond Jared's comprehension and left him reeling over an abundance of unanswered questions. But if he didn't follow the map, how would he make any breaks in the case?

Jared pushed back to lean against the wall and dipped his head between his knees. How long had these affairs been going on, and what was the breaking point that got his friend killed?

Did Halley know about Mark's other women? Did she decide to take matters into her own hands— committing a crime of passion?

His head ached, and his whole body lagged. Shoving the contents back into the envelope, Jared pressed the power button on the phone.

Nothing—probably needed a charge. He dug around. Maybe he could find a fossilized charger for the antique phone somewhere.

The mystery was getting deeper, and he'd left his hip waders at home.

Jared took a quarter from his pocket—Heads, he'd turn in the evidence and take his punishment like a man—tails, he'd follow the lead and play detective. He'd grown up with Mark, and their life chapters converged. He couldn't believe this was happening. A man with two faces had posed as a loyal husband, engineer, and brother.

The quarter soared into the air, spinning wildly from him flicking the edge with his thumb, before landing in his open palm. He lifted his fingers and focused on the eagle staring back at him.

At first light, he'd follow the map. Maybe it would lead him to the answers he so desperately needed, or perhaps, if luck was on his side, the lines would lead him straight to Halley.

****

Bo pulled up to his apartment building and cut the engine. His head dropped to the steering wheel while he simultaneously kicked the door with his booted foot. The mission wasn't supposed to play out like this. Sure, he'd spent years praying for the wrath of God to knock his enemy down a few pegs…maybe he even wished for a complete upheaval. But wishing and acting were two completely different concepts, and he didn't have the will or the balls to take a human life. He never meant for this to happen.

Now his partner looked like a battered fruit, and an innocent woman was on the run. He holstered his weapon and opened the door to his rusty old truck—the only thing he had left from his old life—the one before his family deserted him.

And he had a dead man to thank.

Mark's carelessness set off a chain of events that sent mass destruction roaring through his home.

Bo stepped down onto the pavement and breathed in the night air. How did things get so out of control? Time never stopped ticking away, and he had a matter of days, maybe less, before secrets came to light.

People hoped secrets would die with the dead and stay buried six feet under for the rest of eternity. But more often than not, that's when they worked their way to the surface.

Mark's indiscretions were a can of worms with a cracked lid, and one tap would set them all loose.

Bo might not have been the one to end the bastard's life…but the blood was on his hands. He looked around and yanked open the door to his apartment building. His phone rang. "Hello?"

"Hey, Bo. It's me, Steve." The man chewed loudly on the other end.

Gross. "Steve. Do you think maybe you could hold off eating until after our conversation?"

"Oh, yeah. No problem." A wrapper crinkled, and Steve cleared his throat. "So I asked for the results of your tox screening stat. The missus and I are going to Mexico for a couple of weeks, and I didn't want to leave you hanging."

Bo chuckled under his breath. Sonia had been riding Steve's tail about moving back to Mexico since they married six months ago. He'd be shocked if they ever came back. "What were the results?"

"Well, your victim was definitely drugged with a sedative, a fairly common one."

"Who'd have access to something like that?"

"Anyone. Doctors dole the pills out like candy around here and use the liquid form to calm patients down when they come to the emergency room. They've got a hefty street value too. It won't hurt to ask some local drug dealers if they've dealt with anyone out of the ordinary lately. I mean, if they'll talk to you."

A couple of guys in lock-up might be willing to

talk, but he wouldn't bet his job on anything they said. "That's a great idea. And thanks for getting back to me. Have fun on vacation." Bo lowered the phone, but Steve yelled on the other end. "Did you say something else?"

"Yeah, geez. You in some kind of a hurry?"

"No. Sorry. I just thought we were done." Bo entered his rundown apartment, lifted a lip in disgust at the smoke-stained, peeling wallpaper, and threw his keys onto the cracked granite counter. Mice scurried into the hall as he shut the door. *They* didn't even want to be there. "Anyway, you were saying?"

"We also found a strand of hair, but I left for lunch before I ran it. When I came back, the hair was gone."

"That's bizarre." Bo scratched his head, peeled back the film on his microwave dinner, and set the timer. "Sounds like an inside job to me. Did you check the security cameras to see if anyone went in or out of the room besides you?"

Steve snorted. "The camera above my door has been down for months. I keep putting in work orders, but something else always trumps my camera troubles."

Who in the department besides Jared would give a rat's ass about Mark Martin? "What do you think?"

"You said the words, not me." Steve chewed loudly into the phone again. "I gotta get going. Sonia keeps beeping in, and if I don't answer, she'll make me eat refried beans for dinner again." His voice trembled. "My intestines can't handle that. And neither can my bathroom."

"Thanks again, Steve. I'll talk to you when you get back. Have a safe trip." Bo rubbed his chin. He could let this go. He could let Halley take the fall and move on with his life. Maybe he'd move down south and get the hell out of Dodge before winter hit. He broke the law by blackmailing the man who destroyed his family. There was no question about his misjudgment. But letting an innocent woman spend the rest of her life in prison was different. If Halley was convicted, Jared would go down with her.

His partner's feelings for the woman were written all over his face, even if he didn't admit them yet, and he'd never recover from not being able to save her.

As Bo grabbed his steaming entrée of macaroni and broccoli, his phone rang again. This time he didn't recognize the number. "If this is one of those telemarketing calls, you can kiss my a—"

"You need to mind your own business, Officer Frazer. Why don't you just sit down, enjoy your frozen dinner, and quit sticking your nose where it doesn't belong?" The voice was low and robotic, obviously altered with help from an electronic device.

"Who is this?" Bo walked to his window and peeked out into the lamp-lit streets. "What do you want?"

"I wanted to thank you for showing me what a piece of scum Mark Martin truly was. And don't worry, I got justice for both of us."

"I never showed you anything." Bo growled and closed his blackout curtains.

"You did. You just didn't know it."

The line went dead.

The Carolinas sounded better by the second.

Chapter Five

Halley's uninjured arm hit something solid as she turned. Her eyes fluttered open, and she screamed as the person beside her came into focus.

She found her voice through the shock, but she trembled uncontrollably, her teeth chattering from her panic. "M-Mark?"

"Yeah, baby. It's me. You look beautiful and sexy in my shirt." He smiled at her like he had every other morning they'd woken up together, then kissed her lips sweetly.

Halley stiffened when his lips touched hers. "How is this possible?" He'd been covered in stab wounds, and she'd seen his lifeless body with her own two eyes. Hadn't she? She smoothed down her crisp white shirt. Where was the blood? "No. You aren't really here. You're—"

"Dead?" he whispered. Mark's laugh wasn't sweet like his kiss. His eyes blackened, and splotches of red seeped through the sheet. "Of course, I'm dead. You killed me, remember?"

She scrambled backward as the blood trail chased her. "Mark, I didn't..." Her next words came out as a murmur. At this point, she wasn't even sure she believed them. "I didn't kill you."

Mark pulled the sheet back, revealing the open stab wounds on his chest. His mouth turned down. "You did this." He smacked the mattress. "Who else could've done it? You were with me when I died, and you were the last person to see me alive."

Another voice caught her attention, and the blood in her veins turned to ice.

"Halley, honey. Maybe if you had tried a little harder, you could've saved him."

"Mom?" Halley followed the voice until she saw brown eyes, black hair with silver strands, and a wide, loving grin. "Mom, I thought I would never see you again. I tried so hard to save you, and I-I just couldn't."

"You just didn't try hard enough, sweetheart." She tucked a strand of loose hair behind Halley's ear. "You must not have loved me as much as you claim."

How could she say those things? Her own mother. Halley's legs were glued to the bed, no matter how hard she tried to move them.

She began to turn away, but Mark grasped her tender wrist. She cried out as pain rippled through her arm.

"Don't feel bad, Amelia," Mark said. "She just stared at me. The operator had to remind her about doing CPR before she even started. What a wife. What a killer."

"Mark, let go of me! I swear on my life, I didn't do this to you. I'm not a killer!"

"Liar! Look at me, Halley. Look at what you did!" Mark chuckled, soft at first, but his tone became low and slower, like a man possessed by a demon. His voice was subhuman as he spoke. "You're about to feel what I felt."

Agony rippled up her arm and into her chest as she screwed her eyes shut. The sound of skin tearing and multi-pitched laughing crackled in her ears. Air left her lungs, and when her eyes shot open, she gasped for more.

A dream. Holy shit. Halley's mind was wreaking havoc on her soul. For a moment, she convinced herself she had killed Mark. But that would be crazy, right?

Her uneven breaths left her dizzy and disoriented. "Everything is okay," she crooned, calming herself. "Just a trick of the mind. Not real at all."

She had to get up to brush off the bizarre nightmare. If she didn't, she'd start questioning her sanity—a road no one should ever go down.

Halley's stomach rumbled when she sat up, wincing at the pain in her arm. She squinted at the rusty orange hue of morning light pouring through the window, stood, and examined what she could see of her disgusting appearance, then hobbled over to the pantry. Blisters had formed, and the open wounds on the bottoms of her feet screamed with every step.

Halley swung open the pantry doors and pulled out a long drawer filled to the brim with canned food. Peas, peaches, corn, and *ew*, asparagus—that must've been Mark's. Not the best selection, but beggars couldn't be choosers, and in this scenario, she was the beggar.

After setting a can of peaches on the counter, she knelt and retrieved a gallon jug of water from the bottom shelf. Removing the seal and flipping the top off with her thumb, she lifted the opening to her lips and let the room-temperature water slide down her scratchy hot throat. The refreshing liquid soaked her shirt and trickled to the floor, hints of blood turning the water pink when it pooled on the floor.

Halley wiped the water from her chin and

scrunched her toes in the small puddle forming at her feet.

A ray of light outlined a footprint near where she had passed out the night before—a print identical to the one she accidentally fanned away. The odd chevron pattern wasn't common, and she owned enough shoes to be sure. This one had a mate—a smaller, more feminine one that sure as hell wasn't hers. Carefully, she followed the trail to the bedroom with the gallon jug clutched tight to her chest.

The queen-sized bed was in shambles. Sheets and her handmade quilt lay crumpled in a lump at the foot of the bed.

Halley moved around the edge, bent, and sniffed the pillow. Vanilla?

Her stomach tightened. Almost a year had gone by since she'd been there last. And the only vanilla she liked belonged on top of a cupcake. The scent, the footprints, the bedding—these odd things could only mean one thing.

Mark had been having an affair.

But with who? And for how long?

Son of a bitch. She'd given him her entire adult life, and this was how he repaid her? By sleeping around? She held her breath and released a low, primal growl from somewhere deep and dark—somewhere she'd never been privy to before.

Halley slammed the jug of water onto the end table with such force that droplets escaped over the sides. How dare he? And on the damn sheets she'd picked out herself. She dug her nails into the fitted sheet and stripped the bed like a wild animal before tearing into the pillows like the coyote would've clawed into her if she hadn't gotten away.

Everything hurt. Her arm would barely bend, but the momentary psychotic break was necessary and worth the pain.

She stayed home every day of her life—Mark's little trophy wife and the black-haired, blue-eyed bombshell he showed off to his friends at work parties. With no college education, no family, and no extraordinary skills under her belt, she was the basic definition of useless—widowed and useless.

Well, not anymore.

Halley stormed to the kitchen, ripped open the drawer beneath the sink, and held up a box of matches. Her whole life just went up in flames, and that fucking bed was going to suffer the same fate.

The match fit perfectly between her two fingers. She placed the tip against the striker, and the small flame sprang to life as yellow and orange danced within the blue atop the thin wooden stick. She marveled at the beauty. How could something so stunning be responsible for so much destruction?

The same could be said for her heart. Halley closed her eyes and blew out the match. Letting her pain destroy everything she'd helped Mark build over the years wouldn't change what happened or what he'd done. She could set her entire past ablaze, but then her soul would mirror the burn—wild, hot, unextinguishable—and turn who she was into a pile of ash. Plus, she'd be down a cabin…and she sorta wanted to keep that.

****

Jared moaned. Getting dressed had been a nightmare as he struggled to lift his arms and bend after sleeping in an awkward position all night.

Mark had highlighted three separate lines, and about thirty miles existed between each one.

Jared left his house before daybreak and started at the top. The first line led him to an up-and-coming housing development. He drove around the connected circles, looking for a sign of something tangible, but there were only backhoes, heavy machinery, and dirt with a wooden sign at the entrance.

The second route had also been a fake-out, leading him to a condemned restaurant with weeds pushing their way through the cracked pavement. But the last line was the charm.

When he'd turned down the dirt road, memories of fishing in the river at the bottom of the ravine invaded his mind. They'd fished there every weekend as kids and dubbed the spot their happy place. When they were fishing, Jared wasn't getting hit, and Mark could catch a break from his overbearing mother's perfectionist demands. All families had their fair share of problems, but both of them got screwed in the parental department.

Mark's mother was probably culpable for his infidelities, at least partially. The only thing she ever taught him was to find faults at every turn and never be satisfied with anything—even though she was far from perfect herself.

Jared had driven slowly down the narrow road and stopped where a large section of metal was missing from the guard rail. He'd almost driven past the opening due to it being camouflaged by overgrown grass and shadows from the trees. He backed up and pointed the car's front end toward the entrance and peered down over the steep embankment. The path looked barely wide enough to host two hikers, let alone one full-sized vehicle, but the time was now or never, and *never* didn't sit right with him.

Jared gave the car a little gas before letting off the pedal, rolling down the hill with little more than gravitational pull. Before he hit bottom, he punched the gas and laughed maniacally as the car flew up the other side, like a top-of-the-line roller coaster, bottoming out six times before the trail came to a point, ending abruptly. Had he hit another dead end? The landscape was thick and dense, but there was no way he'd taken a wrong turn.

He killed the engine and rubbed his throbbing ribs before starting out on foot.

Ten, maybe fifteen, minutes passed, and then he stumbled upon a mixture of human and animal prints scattered throughout the dirt and mud. He followed them for another minute or two before looking up.

A humble-looking cabin with a tin roof matching the color of the surrounding pines caught his eye.

Pale-yellow shutters offset the dark logs that formed the cabin's frame. Quaint, yet still probably cost more money than he made in a year.

A blurry streak ran past the window, and he took the steps cautiously. Not just because he didn't want to scare Halley off if she was inside, but because his ribs had gone from throbbing to searing. By the time he reached the porch, his side burned like a wildfire begging to be extinguished.

Jared knocked for a small eternity. He lifted the round silver knocker and let it fall one more time.

No response.

He jiggled the handle, and the knob turned. He gave the door a light nudge and stood at the threshold like a vampire waiting for an invitation. Before his boot could cross the barrier, a shrill battle cry exploded from his left.

A sharp pain ran down his face, and an awkward noise reverberated in his ear. His back hit the porch when his knees gave out, and he groaned in agony.

"What the fuck was that?" He pressed a hand to the side of his head, and blood trickled down his cheek for the second time in less than twenty-four hours. Excellent. Because a car accident and two broken ribs weren't enough.

Halley panted above him.

He almost didn't recognize the feral, dirty, wild-eyed woman standing above him, gripping a stainless-steel pot like her life depended on it. Honestly, he couldn't say the woman was Halley with one hundred percent certainty.

"Halley?"

Mud streaked across her cheek, and pieces of dead leaves clung to the loose, greasy strands of her hair.

"Is that you?"

"You shouldn't have come here, Jared. I don't need or want you here."

"I can't believe you hit me with a freakin' pot."

"Guess you should've stayed home, then."

"I'm just trying to help you."

Halley lifted the pot above her head. "I already told you. I don't want *your* help."

"Yeah. You've made that pretty clear." He propped himself up using his elbows, wiped the blood from his fingers onto his jeans, and gazed around the inside.

69

"What is this place anyway? Mark never mentioned this place—not once. How long has the cabin been here?"

Halley's arms fell, and she set her weapon on the ground, holding out her free hand. "We built the base a few years ago, then finished the rest about a year later. I was specifically instructed never to mention the cabin to anyone...not even you."

Jared accepted her hand and heaved himself off the floor, trying his best not to put too much strain on Halley's fragile frame. "Probably because that moron built it illegally. This cabin is on national forest grounds, which means government land, which means you can't put up a building without proper permits and permissions. I'm guessing, considering all the secrecy, that Mark had none of those things. *When* they find this place, they'll bulldoze it to the ground."

She shrugged. "Yeah, well, Mark neglecting to mention things seems to be a trending theme lately."

"What do you mean?"

Halley grabbed the pot and fixed her grip. "Just forget about everything—this, me, the cabin, everything. Because, if you're here to take me to jail, you're gonna have to take me in a body bag." She straightened. "I'm not leaving until I get to the bottom of this."

"Put the pan down, crazy. I'm not here to arrest you...yet. Don't you think I want to figure this shit out too? Besides, you're about one strong wind gust away from falling over." He pointed to her arm. "And that club you got there is twice the size of your other arm." He reached over and ripped the pan from her hand. "You couldn't kill an ant right now, by the looks of ya. Now, go sit at the table and relax."

Halley wobbled to the table. "Go to the table," she mocked. "How did you find this place, anyway? Nobody's supposed to know about it. Mark always said if things went bad, we'd be safe here." Snort. "Well, things are bad, and here I am." She squinted at him. "Whether I'm safe or not has yet to be determined."

"I'm not here to hurt you, and I know what happened yesterday between you and me was shitty, but you have to understand…" Jared paused and wandered around the kitchen, opening cupboards until he found a washrag. "Do you have running water here?"

"No. There's an open jug of water in the bedroom, and we have the creek down back if you need more than that. Now, how about answering my question?"

"I'm getting to that. Anyway, as I was saying, I'm sorry about putting you into a cop car, but there was so much confusion, and I-I just went a little bit nuts. I'd be lying if I said all the unanswered questions didn't raise suspicion, but I'm trying my best to look at the facts and not my feelings." He strolled to the bedroom, snagged the jug from the nightstand, took one look at the jacked-up bed, and headed back to the kitchen. "Did you let a bobcat into your bed?" He chuckled as he poured the water over the rag, but when he peered over at her, Halley's face was sheet white. "It was just a joke, Halley. Here, take this and wipe yourself down until I can get more water from the creek." He handed her the soaked rag.

"I'm sorry, I just…"

"Wait, did you really have a bobcat in there?"

"No. I was chased down by a coyote last night. I almost didn't make it, but I knew I had to. I just kept running and running without looking back. He looked skinny, so I think quite a while had passed since he'd eaten last. He was limping too, so he must've had a bad leg. Most likely that was the only reason I was able to outrun him."

Jared's heart sank to his stomach. "Jesus, Halley. I'm so sorry. I had no idea."

"How could you have? And then this morning, I found out that Mark was…" She lowered her head, and droplets fell from her eyes to her bare legs.

"Found out what?" Jared gingerly crouched and lifted her chin. "Answer me. Please."

"Mark was having an affair."

So, she didn't know about the affairs when Mark was murdered. At least now, when he broke the news that there was more than one affair, the sting wouldn't burn as bad. He hoped.

"How did you find out?"

"I found a bunch of footprints in the dust—a man's and a woman's. I haven't been up here in a long time, so they definitely weren't mine. Plus, the bed was in complete shambles, and the pillow smelled like vanilla, and I *hate* vanilla in perfume."

Time was running out. If Mark had brought his mistresses up here, then they weren't as secluded as they thought.

"Listen, I didn't want to tell you in such a blunt manner, but Mark's infidelities went way beyond one woman, one time. I went back to check your house for more clues, but someone attacked me. They had covered their face with a mask, wore all black, and side-checked me. The whole thing was a blur. They ended up getting away, but I think I found what they were searching for." Jared shrugged. "The grandfather clock in your hallway had a false bottom, and there was a packet of photos and an old-ass cell phone inside."

Halley wiped the tears from her cheeks with the washrag, but the dirt only moved farther down her face. "We've covered the fact that my dead husband was a cheating bastard, but that still doesn't explain how you found me."

"There was a map behind all the photos. Mark did a good job of leading me in the wrong direction...I'll give him that. Finding this place took me forever."

"It was probably drawn up by one of his whores." Halley sat up straight and smacked the wet cloth off the table. "Wait a minute."

"What?"

"I didn't kill Mark, but someone did, right?"

"Uh. Right." Where was she going with this?

"Well, now we have some suspects."

"How do you figure?"

"Because. A woman scorned is a dangerous thing. Hell, Mark's lucky I didn't find out about his affairs beforehand. I might have killed him myself."

Jared sighed. "You don't mean that, Halley. I don't think you have the killing gene." He leaned against the table and drummed his fingers. "Are you implying that one of the women he was sleeping with killed him?"

She smiled. "Exactly! We just have to figure out which one, and why?"

Jared pulled out a chair and sat. The release relaxed his ribs and eased the aching in his back. "What do you mean, why? They probably found out about the other women too. You said it yourself, a woman scorned..."

"Yeah, but I have a feeling there's more to this than meets the eye." Halley pulled a crisp leaf from her hair. "Mark would've had to push one of them past the breaking point—more than a measly affair—driving them to kill. No way. This goes deeper than we know."

"Yeah." Jared cleared his throat. "There's just one teensy problem. I'm *technically* not involved with the case anymore."

Halley raised an eyebrow. "But you're one of the best officers they've got."

"Funny, Captain Maxwell said the same exact thing right before he suspended me. My relationship with you and Mark created a conflict of interest, so he assigned Bo and Stan Cordini to the case."

Her sly grin sent a hot bolt through his lower stomach. The feeling wasn't new but was one he needed to ignore. This thing—the back-and-forth they always shared—would never amount to anything other than mutual friendship and respect. Otherwise, he'd be the bad guy.

"I guess we'll just have to solve this before they do—on the down-low, of course. And when we find the murderer, my name will be free and clear." She bowed in her chair. "That, my friend, is how you kill two birds with one stone."

What did he have to lose—besides his badge, house, and everything meaningful in his life? Being stripped of his badge would follow him like a plague— a scuff on his good name. Jared could live with a soiled reputation, but losing Halley would be unbearable. He stole the washrag from her and wiped the dirt from her forehead while attempting to remove clumps of moss from her hair.

"I don't know how the hell you talked me into your asinine scheme using skewed logic, but if we're going to work this case together, we're going play by my rules. Understand?"

Halley jumped up and wrapped her good arm around Jared's neck, placing a soft kiss on his cheek. "I understand."

****

She should've guessed Halley would come here. And why wouldn't she? Smart little bitch. If the woman could get past the lack of electricity and running water, she could hide here for months, if not longer.

Nestling herself halfway behind a large maple tree, she pulled out a pair of high-powered binoculars. Her lovestruck minion had been kind enough to hand them over without much fuss. Maybe she could sell them when she finished; some extra money to get out of town would be nice.

She aimed the binoculars at the window and studied the interaction between Halley and Jared, intrigued by the unmistakable chemistry between them.

She snorted as he wiped down Halley's disgusting face. "I'll be damned," she whispered to the forest. "He's in love with her. What a disgrace." That revelation could make things a tad more complicated.

After Jared tried to break her leg last night, she had hobbled home, pissed off by her own incompetence. Retrieve the envelope, phone, and map—erase all evidence from existence. She couldn't even do that correctly. However, she wasn't a failure on all counts. Mark was dead, and she'd call that a win.

When Jared left in the ugly orange taxi, she snuck back in, but everything was gone.

Her picture was in that stack. The angle hid her face, but she had something the other women didn't, and when Jared looked close, which he always did, he'd identify her.

She lowered the binoculars and pressed her back against the tree's strong trunk, letting her ass sink to the ground. Mark had said he loved her. He said they'd spend the rest of their lives together, but he lied.

How dare he throw her away like garbage?

What kind of man bowed to a little blackmail?

Seeing Mark tangled up with those other women blew her ego to bits, but she would've forgiven him. They could've worked things out. He should've let that broken cop tell Halley everything, then they could've started a new life together, but no...poor, innocent Halley's heart was too fragile.

She didn't give a hoot about how fragile the bitch's heart was. The softer the organ, the easier it could be destroyed.

Mark's broken promises weren't even the worst part. After discovering what he did, she had no other choice. She had to kill him.

Chapter Six

Halley finger combed her damp hair and wrapped the plush green towel around her breasts, tucking the towel's corner tightly between them. Her feet pulsated, and her arm had tripled in size. But at least most of the dirt and grime was gone.

She'd used both pails of water Jared had brought in from the creek. Layers of earth melted from her body onto the floor of the galvanized basin and swirled down the drain. If only every problem could be solved with soap and water. There was no way the temp could've been over forty degrees, but freezing was a small price to pay to feel human again.

She grabbed the lantern off the hook in the ceiling, pressed the towel tight against her chest, and headed back to the bedroom. But she wasn't alone.

Jared sat on the bed, messing with the sheets she'd destroyed earlier. His legs were bent over the edge, feet planted firmly on the floor.

She watched him for a moment. Maybe she should've been startled or put off by his presence on the bed she'd shared with Mark.

They'd only made love in those sheets once, but the memory still sent butterflies to the pit of her stomach. After everything she'd learned, the flutters pissed her off more than anything else. So why should shame warm her cheeks at the jolt to her center when she saw Jared in her room? He seemed to fit in with the chaos surrounding them, which scared her even more.

She walked around the bed and stood in front of him.

He stopped tussling with the shredded sheets, and his gaze roamed her body before he abruptly went back to his project. "I'm sorry. I should've done this at the kitchen table. I wasn't thinking."

"It's okay. Not a big deal." But it was. The fact that he was in her bedroom while she stood there clad only in a towel was secretly thrilling…and terrifying. Why wasn't she mortified? More importantly, why wasn't she asking him to leave?

Jared gathered up a bundle of odds and ends off the bed and lifted them to his chest. "I'll, uh, just finish this in the other room."

Halley nodded and kept her eyes glued to all six-foot-three inches of him as he walked away.

Her stomach quivered, and a pang of guilt slapped her like a scorned mistress.

Oh, the irony.

Mark had aroused her, but in a Prince Charming sort of way. He always knew what to say and how to get out of anything using just his words. And he *always* saved the day. As proven by Mark's harem, plenty of other women had felt the same way. *Asshole.*

On the other hand, Jared straddled the line between dependable and dangerous. A good ole boy with a huge heart who dished out fierce loyalty. He'd kill for the ones he loved. She didn't doubt his intentions. Then again, she'd never questioned her husband's intentions either, and look where that got her.

Halley rolled her eyes, brushing her internal

dialogue to the wayside. She crouched low to remove the airtight tote full of clothes from underneath the bed frame and cinched the towel tighter, sneezing half a dozen times as plumes of dust snuck into her nose.

"Everything all right in there?" Jared hollered from the kitchen.

She sniffled. "Fine. I just found a dust bunny the size of Texas in here."

"Well, don't let the damn thing eat you. We can't afford any more problems."

She rolled her eyes. Jared couldn't go ten minutes with being sarcastic—a trait she always found a bit pretentious. Deep down, though, she'd always sorta envied his *I don't give a crap* attitude and quick wit.

She opened the bin lid and unfolded her black leggings. The clothes reeked of mothballs and dryer sheets, so she shook them out before putting them on

They were looser than she'd expected, but lack of food would do that to a person. The neck part dug into her throat when she forced the gray sweatshirt over her head. She gripped the center with both hands and yanked until the fabric tore, creating a small slit.

Freshly dressed, she joined Jared at the kitchen table. "What are you making?"

Sticks and shredded pieces of sheet scattered the area. "I'm making a splint for your arm. The swelling has gotten worse, and you're using it way too much. This will keep everything stationary until we can get you seen by a doctor."

"That might be a while."

Jared nodded. "I know, but this should help. I can do a grocery-store run later and pick you up some pain medication and something to eat."

"I have food here. You don't have to buy any."

Frustration laced his tone as he grabbed her arm and folded her fingers over to form a fist. He positioned her arm just below her breasts. "Come on, Halley. You can't live on peaches and canned vegetables. I've known you for a long time, and never once have I seen you eat asparagus."

Halley winced as Jared placed a smooth stick on each side of her arm and yelped when he tightened the sheet strips in place. "Ow, dammit! Do you have to be so rough?"

"I do if you want to feel better. Now just hold still and stop being a big baby."

Who was he to call her a baby? She'd like to see him outrun a coyote and trek twenty miles. She bit down on her lower lip so she wouldn't punch him in the face.

"After this"—Jared wound the strips of cloth around the makeshift splint—"I thought we could check out the cell phone and see if there're any clues in there. What do you think?"

"I suppose we can't avoid the inevitable. We have to go through everything at some point. Might as well be nowww—oww!" Halley jumped from her chair. The excruciating pain from Jared's final tightening made her sweat like she'd run a marathon. So much for being clean.

Jared patted her leg. "There. All done, champ. If I had a sticker, I'd give you one."

"Ha-ha, smartass." Halley squeezed her shoulder, hoping to work out some of the pain. "Just turn on the phone and let's get this over with."

"Yes, ma'am." Jared pushed the power button, but

the screen stayed black.

What if the battery was junk? What if this piece-of-crap phone held all the answers, but they couldn't get to them? Panic stuck in her throat. "Why isn't it working?"

"Just wait a minute, Hal. The device is older than the dinosaurs and kinda makes you wonder…" Jared stopped and sealed his lips.

She didn't need a psychic to read his thoughts. "Makes you wonder how long Mark was sneaking around behind my back?"

Jared dropped his head. "Yeah. I mean, they haven't sold phones like this for years." His leg bounced under the table. "No. That didn't come out right. There's always the possibility he bought the phone online and didn't wanna spend a fortune."

An awkward silence filled the room.

"I'm just going to stop talking now." He tapped the screen. "Come on, you fossil, just work!" He slammed the phone onto the table, and it lit up like a Christmas tree. "Hallefreakinluja!"

"Can I see the phone?" Halley held out her hand. Mark was her husband, and she had every right to look at the phone before Jared. She'd never be the last to know again. "Please?"

Jared set the small black electronic device in her hand but kept his fingers wrapped around the chipped plastic. "Before you go poking around, just remember that there's no proof this phone is Mark's. For all we know, this could be the killer's."

She nodded, and he released.

No passcode existed. Not very smart, in her opinion. People who lead double lives behind their wives' backs should probably use a passcode. Halley clicked on the tiny square that said *PHOTOS* and scrolled through the lineup. Her stomach knotted as if someone had stuck their hand down her throat and squeezed.

There were pictures upon pictures of Mark with women from all different walks of life. Some blonde, some brunette, some thick, and some not. He'd been a busy boy. Something about the way he took these photos sent a shiver down her spine. None of the images showed the women's faces, and he'd either taken them from behind or from the chest down. Did these women mean so little to him, or was he really worried she might find out about what he'd been doing? Were they women she knew? Is that why he never showed their faces?

Her lip trembled. Facing reality was more complicated than she thought.

The videos were in a separate folder. Her heart jumped, and her mouth went dry. The timestamp at the top was the day before he returned from Colorado.

Halley hit Play.

A long-legged blonde, wrapped in a fuzzy white robe, lay flat on top of what looked like a motel room bed.

Again, Halley couldn't see her face.

The door next to the bed opened, and a male entered the room in the same robe. The quality of the video was dismal and grainy.

The man dropped his robe, and any shred of innocence she'd held onto about her husband vanished. The birthmark on Mark's ass that looked like the outline of a dog became visible.

Halley kept watching until he climbed on top of the svelte blonde. Enough was enough. She flipped the phone over and shook her head. She didn't ask for this, but someone else's poor choices were thrown in her lap, and now she had to face the aftermath. Unfair wasn't a strong-enough word.

"Well?" Jared asked. "Is the phone Mark's?"

"Uh, yeah. I'm pretty sure. You can go through everything if you want." Halley rose from her spot at the table. "I'm gonna go lie down for a minute. Okay?" She didn't wait for a reply because she didn't want him to see her cry again. Dragging her exhausted and aching body to the bedroom, she plopped down onto the disastrous bed and allowed the tears to fall freely. Betrayal crept up like a midnight monster, and she had no choice but to relinquish everything she thought she knew about *forever*—something she'd been promised and not given.

He'd promised to love her—to be faithful until death parted them.

She'd held up her end of the bargain, and the loyalty landed her here with a one-way ticket to pay for his mistakes. She couldn't remain disillusioned any longer, and the spot of empathy and love she'd saved in her heart for Mark now had a vacancy. At this point, she'd sell it to the highest bidder for a fucking candy bar.

Halley's eyelids lowered—heavy with exhaustion and an inability to deal with her current situation. The world around her went dark. After a few hours, things would be better.

She would be better.

****

Jared had checked on her at least a hundred times throughout the night and early morning, but noon was creeping up fast, and she'd been asleep for almost a full day. If Halley hadn't been a suspected murderer and his ass wasn't on the line for aiding and abetting a felon, time wouldn't be so precious.

While she slept, he'd sifted through the phone for more clues. And after going through the photos and videos, he wholeheartedly understood why Halley had retired to the bedroom so suddenly. He could hear her trying to stifle her cries before she passed out, and her pain tore him up inside. How did neither of them ever catch on to Mark's schemes? How in the hell did the man lead a totally separate life without ever being found out?

Mark was good. So good that Jared questioned if he ever truly knew his best friend at all.

He cracked the bedroom door. He'd always appreciated Halley's beauty, but until recently, he'd ignored his feelings. He stood in the doorway and watched her chest rise and fall. He reveled in the jet-black locks winding across the pillow like vines, momentarily wishing he could run his fingers through them.

Guilt was a bitch. Even though Halley was now technically single, she was still his best-friend's wife. The last thing he wanted to do was complicate her life more than Mark had already done. That just wouldn't be fair. He brushed off the lust and strolled to the bed, then shook Halley lightly.

"Hal. Halley. Time to wake up." Jared switched on the lantern.

She turned her head away from the light. "What

time is it? How long have I been sleeping?"

He sat beside her. "You've been out for almost twenty-four hours. It's pushing noon."

Halley shot up. "Seriously? Why did you let me sleep so long?"

Jared chuckled. He couldn't help but laugh at how disheveled she looked—like she'd just woken up after an all-night drinking bender. He'd participated in a few of those back in the day, and the next morning was about as pretty as a train wreck.

"Trust me. You needed the rest, and some of the color's even come back to your cheeks." He froze. "Not that I was looking…I mean, I just, you were kinda pale."

Halley raised her eyebrows. "I get your point, Jared. I looked like crap yesterday."

Well, he'd met his quota of embarrassment for the day. He headed toward the door. "Just meet me in the kitchen when you're ready. I found some more clues we might be able to follow."

Shutting the door behind him, he hung his head in shame. *Good one, you dip. She probably thinks you've been watching her sleep all night. But you were. Oh my God, you've turned into a creeper. You've literally arrested guys for watching women sleep before.* He slapped himself on the forehead and seated himself back at the table.

Halley stepped out of the bedroom. "Thanks for putting some more water in the bathroom for me. It felt good to wash my face this morning…or afternoon?" She glared out the window. "Screw it. I'm done keeping track of time." She shuffled to the table and sat. "You know, I would kill for some coffee right about now."

"You're not the only one. I'm pretty sure caffeine withdrawal is the cause of this nagging headache." Jared pulled a napkin from his pocket and slid the white square across the table.

"What's this?" She squinted at the napkin.

"They are recently dialed and received numbers from Mark's phone. Do you recognize any of them? I noticed one number has a local area code."

Halley's eyes bulged as she scanned to the bottom of the list.

"What's wrong? Did you see a number you recognize?"

She turned the napkin to face him and pointed to the one local number at the bottom. "I know this one. It's a pay phone."

Jared cleared his throat. "I don't mean to pry, but how in the hell do you know the number to a pay phone?"

"I used to use this one all the time after my parents died." Halley lowered her head and closed her eyes.

Jared swooped into the chair beside her and took her hand. "I know talking about your parents is hard for you, but I need you to push through the pain. This could be a big break for us."

"Well, after my parents died, I ended up at a foster home near Colson Bridge, which is where the pay phone is. I snuck out one night and was walking by the pay phone when it rang. So in typical curious teenage fashion, I answered the call. The lady on the other end sounded older and had dialed the wrong number. Her voice was so similar to my mom's that I just broke down and started bawling. After she got me settled, she told me she'd call the pay phone every night at the same time to talk to me. She said when I stopped answering, she'd stop calling."

"Jesus, Halley. I had no idea things were so hard for you. I wish I'd known you then. Maybe I could've helped you."

Halley grazed her hand along his stubble. "There was nothing you could've done to make me feel better back then. I have you now, and that's all that matters."

Something happened, and his body moved without permission. He wrapped his hand around the back of Halley's neck and pulled her mouth to his. Her lips tasted of peppermint, but her skin smelled like honey. Alarms buzzed in his head, warning him to pull back, but Halley's lips parted, and he hardened at her soft moans.

Too fast—way too fast.

Jared released her and turned, focusing on slowing his rapid breaths. "We can't do this, Halley. I want you more than I've ever wanted anything, but you're my best friend's wife. Mark's only been gone for two days, and here I am, pawing at his leftovers."

He'd just said a bad, bad thing, and even he wasn't quite sure where the words came from. He hated himself for wanting Halley, and he despised the fact he couldn't control himself around her. "I didn't mean to say that. All I meant was—"

Halley met his gaze, pulled her hand back, and slapped him across the face. "Don't you ever tell me what I can and cannot do. I'm not a leftover or a side dish like broccoli. I didn't accept your kiss to get back at my husband for his infidelities. I accepted your kiss because I like you, enjoy your company, and feel something for you that I haven't felt in a long, long time. And let's get one thing straight. I *was* Mark's wife." Halley pointed her finger at his nose. "Do I make myself clear?"

"Yes, ma'am."

Halley rubbed her hand on her black leggings. "Good. Now, are you still planning on going to the grocery store today?"

He'd never seen this side of her before—confident and in charge. Halley's alpha female vibrato was sexy and slightly intimidating. None of that changed what he'd done. He kissed her. He kissed his murdered best friend's wife, and there was a special place in hell for men like him. The status of their marriage didn't matter. His actions were unforgivable. Still, Mark didn't deserve a woman like Halley. That much was clear. "Yes, that's the plan."

"Good. Give me five minutes, and I'll ride down with you."

Jared scoffed. "You can't be serious. Every police officer in Charlotte is looking for you. You're not going."

"Um. Didn't I just tell you in very simple terms that you are in no way, shape, or form the boss of me?"

"You did. But you also agreed to do things my way."

Halley shrugged. "Agreements can be amended."

Of course they can.

Chapter Seven

Cars packed the main lot at the grocery store.

Jared maneuvered through the lot to the side of the loading dock while Halley sat quietly in the front seat, trying to avoid small talk at all costs. Not like she had anything to say…her lips had done most of the talking for her back at the cabin.

Stupid lips.

She studied his hands as they turned the steering wheel, his movements careful and precise. "Do they teach you to drive like this at the academy?"

"Why? You like my mad driving skills?" Jared laughed and pulled in beside a pair of dumpsters with flies swarming near the lids.

"I was trying to give you a compliment, but if you're going to be smug, then I rescind my praise."

"Nope. No take-backs allowed. But to answer your question, yes, they do teach precision driving at the academy."

Halley nodded and looked out her window. "Nice." Well, her pledge to keep quiet lasted approximately six seconds. If she superglued her lips shut, maybe she'd make it to ten. "Uh, yeah. I guess learning how to lose a tail is pretty cool."

"A tail?"

"Yeah, you know. Like if someone's following you." The conversation had finally moved into the much more tolerable chatter territory. "Has anyone ever *tailed* you before?"

"Actually, yes."

"Seriously?" Halley shifted in her seat and folded her legs like a pretzel. "What happened?"

Jared cut the engine and looked around. "I've never told anyone this, but after my first night on the job, I was driving home from the precinct, and I noticed a car mirroring my every turn. So I just randomly went down a few side streets, thinking it might be a coincidence, but they kept on for a couple more miles." He sighed and shoved the car keys into his pocket.

"Then what happened?"

"No." He waved his hand and shook his head. "You might get scared."

"I will not. Come on. Pleeease?" She scooched closer to the center console.

"This story is not for the faint of heart." He looked around and crooked his finger for her to lean in. "Are you sure you want to hear the rest?"

Her nervous system took over, Jared's question forcing her to think hard about her answer. "Uh, yeah. I'm invested at this point."

"I thought you might say that." His fingers dug into the console as he crossed the imaginary boundary line.

What was happening? His hot breath on her ear caused a stir in a spot that should be unaffected.

He gently caressed her free arm and pushed her wrist back.

Something cold brushed across Halley's skin, and she shivered. She waited a beat to see where Jared's story was heading.

"Boo," he whispered and laughed.

She gasped and jerked back, unsure if she'd been scared by his word or the close proximity.

Jared crossed back over the barrier and cocked his head to the side. "Whoa. Settle down, Halley. Are you okay? I was just messing around a bit, trying to lighten the mood. I'm sorry if I scared you."

"I-I'm fine. You don't have anything to be sorry for." She rested her forehead against the window. "I don't know what got into me." Her face burned like she'd been lying under the scorching-hot sun for hours. She was acting like a scaredy cat—like a frightened child—and the vulnerability had left her exposed.

Halley hated being so weak, but after living under Mark's umbrella of what she thought was protection, her guard had fallen, and she'd become someone she didn't recognize or even like. The old Halley would find the present one obnoxious and meek—a far cry from whom she used to be.

Moving from foster home to foster home had thickened her skin. That life didn't offer any other choice, especially when the family was less than loving. But the safety and contentment Mark had offered on that fateful day turned her into poultry—uncooked, wrinkly poultry.

Damn him. No, scratch that. Double damn him.

Maybe he made her useless on purpose so she'd never leave, or maybe she was the one who bent. She'd morphed into this unrecognizable woman with a title that could only be described as a housekeeper with benefits. Did she do it so he wouldn't leave her out in the cold? Well, she sure was freezing now.

Flies swarmed the open dumpster lid, and her stomach gurgled. She was so hungry she seriously debated crawling into the dumpster just to see what all the *buzz* was about. Halley chuckled. Oh God. She was losing her mind. What came next? Delirium? Death?

Halley's fear of going crazy wasn't the only thing wearing on her fragile nerves. She looked over at Jared, who stared back.

The kiss. It'd left her flustered and, for some reason, slightly annoyed. She didn't push him away when he'd pressed his lips to hers; yet he had the nerve to call her a leftover. But part of her wanted him to kiss her again. Therein lay the problem.

"Alrighty then." He sighed, reaching for the handle. "Is there anything you need besides a wrap for your arm and some pain medication?"

Ice cream sounded heavenly, but Mark had never hooked up electricity to the cabin. All she had to make food on was an old wood cooker he picked up at a garage sale. Her sweet tooth ached, but she'd just have to settle for the next best thing. "A candy bar, please. The one with all the nuts and caramel."

"Gross. I hate those ones."

"Good. More for me." She grinned.

Jared opened the door, his expression serious and stoic. "I won't be in there long. You need to lie low until I come out. Lay your head on the center console and stay out of sight. Got it?"

"Yeah, I got it." Halley waited for him to shut the door before slinking down in the seat and resting her head on the hard plastic console.

Cabin fever was getting to her...literally. She missed being able to go to the grocery store or salon. Hell, she even missed shopping for clothes, even though she dreaded having to try them on.

At least three days before any significant shopping trips, Halley would relegate her handy-dandy donut stash to the top cupboard just so her jeans would button. Then, after she got home, she'd down a pint of ice cream, watch reality television for two days, and return all the clothes she just bought because the five pounds of junk food weight snuck up and bit her in the ass.

God. She'd give her left boob for a pint of clunky monkey swirl right about now.

Halley searched the car for something to keep her occupied. Mark's cursed cell phone lay on Jared's seat. She should just leave it alone, but curiosity got the better of her. She cradled the phone and scrolled through the call log. She must have mentioned that pay phone to Mark a million times throughout their marriage. That had to be how he got the idea to use the booth as a booty-call stall, the skeevy bastard.

Something about the times jumped out at her. The calls to and from that pay phone all came between 2:00 and 2:15 every day. Halley looked at the time in the corner of the screen. 2:07. What were the odds?

Peeking just above the dashboard, she could see the bridge on the other side of the river. All she had to do was take the bike trail to the river's edge and connect to the bridge. If she moved quickly, she could be back before Jared returned. And if she didn't, they better dig another hole at the cemetery because he'd definitely kill her.

Halley twisted her hair, shoved the wad underneath Jared's Charlotte PD ball cap, and pulled the brim down to eyebrow level. Next, she stole his aviators from the visor and pushed them up the bridge of her nose. She repositioned the collar of her jacket high around her neck, stepped out of the car, and bolted to the bike path, clutching the evidence inside her pocket.

The sheer insanity of her plan trudged to the forefront of her mind. And the rational side of her brain begged her to go back. Still, she needed to know, and she deserved answers.

****

Halley stood at the far end of the bridge and watched a short-haired brunette in maroon hospital scrubs pace impatiently in front of the pay phone. She couldn't have been more than twenty-three or twenty-four, and judging by the roundness of her protruding belly, she was within days of giving birth.

Reality settled in as Halley pressed her back against the cement barrier. Lowering her body to the pavement, she pressed the number on the screen and brought the phone to her ear. If this was Mark's baby, then this woman had a right to know she'd be raising the child alone.

Ring. Ring.

The young woman picked up without hesitation. "Hello? Mark, is that you?"

Halley covered her mouth, stifling the urge to scream.

"Mark, can you hear me? It's Suzanne. Listen, if you can hear me, I need some money for Lanie. I still don't have a crib yet, and my due date is tomorrow. Mark? Mark?"

Halley gasped. Lanie? The name had haunted their lives for the past seven years. She shivered, thinking back to the trial that almost ended them. No. There was no time for a trip down memory lane. This woman—the mother of her husband's child was the present, and she needed to know the truth.

Gathering her strength, she steadied her voice and lowered her hand, speaking softly. "Mark is dead, Suzanne. He died two days ago. I'm sorry."

"Who is this? If this is some kind of sick joke, I'll—"

"This is Mark's wife, Halley Martin, and I promise you, it's not a joke. I wish I had more time to explain. Just take care of yourself and your baby, okay?"

"You're lying! Mark isn't married. His wife is dead."

"You can believe what you want, Suzanne, but Mark isn't coming back, and I'm very much alive."

"But I…he said…"

"He said a lot of things."

Suzanne whimpered and looked around frantically. She dropped the phone and waddled to a beat-up old car at the opposite end of the bridge, stopping to search the area one more time before driving away.

Halley's heart slowed. She had no more disappointment left, and she truly wished the best for Suzanne and Lanie. Hopefully, they'd find someone to take good care of them.

The phone dangled loosely between her fingers as she hung over the rail above the water. This phone had caused more damage in one day than the murder, car wreck, coyote chase, and six-hour trek to the cabin combined. Halley let the phone slip from her fingers and watched the device all the way down. A boulder lifted from her shoulders as the murky water swallowed it whole.

One tie at a time, Halley. One tie at a time.

****

Panic struck him like a runaway train when Jared got to the car, only to find an empty seat. Thirty minutes. All he'd asked her to do was lie low for thirty damn minutes. Was that really too much to ask?

He combed every inch of the parking lot for any trace of Halley.

Nothing.

Jared sat on the driver's seat, opened a water bottle, and downed two painkillers to treat the pulsating in his ribcage. He let his head fall to the steering wheel and tried to slow his erratic breaths. Suddenly, the car door swung open, and Halley jumped inside.

"Ready to go?" she asked.

He stared at her blankly for a moment, taking in the familiar ball cap on her head and his favorite sunglasses hiding her eyes. If she were a man, he'd have slapped them right off her face. "Where the fuck have you been? I've been out here for ten minutes, having a small cluster of mini-strokes while you're out there doing what? I mean, seriously, Halley, what were you thinking?" His voice rose. "You're a fugitive wanted for the murder of your husband! Do you not understand the severity of this situation, or do you just not care?" He gripped his chest. "Jesus, I think I'm having a heart attack."

Halley threw the cap into the backseat and put his shades back where they belonged. "I got bored and—"

"And what? Went for a nice stroll through the park? Decided to check out the scenery on this lovely fall day?"

"You don't have to be mean. I've been cooped up for two days, going over and over every detail of my life up until this point. Jared, I'm trying to figure this all out. I want my life back—my freedom." Halley touched his leg. "Maybe walking off wasn't my best idea, but when I was lying here looking through Mark's phone, I realized something."

Jared scratched the back of his neck and handed her two pills and water. "First off, I'm sorry. I didn't mean to be so harsh. But this is serious, Hal. If they find you, I can't protect you anymore. You scared the living daylights out of me, and I don't want to lose you too."

Halley tossed the pills into her mouth, took a swig of water, and swallowed. "I'm not going anywhere. I'm sorry too."

Jared started the car. "So. Are you going to tell me what you found?

"That depends on if you let me eat that chicken you bought, right now."

He shot her an awkward glance. "Uh. Nobody eats in my car. And how did you know I bought chicken?"

Halley wiggled in her seat. "I can smell it. Please, please, please?"

Rolling his eyes, he reached back and brought the bag to the front. "Just don't make a mess. I just had her detailed. Now, tell me what you know."

"Well," she said, shoving a massive piece of chicken into her mouth. "I noticed all the calls to and from the pay phone were timestamped around 2:15."

How did he miss that? "Go on."

"I cut through the bike path and saw a younger woman in maroon scrubs waiting by the phone. When I called the number, she picked up and asked Mark to give her money for Lanie."

"Lanie? Who's Lanie?"

Her chewing slowed at his question. "Lanie is Mark's unborn child. But Suzanne, that's his mistress's name, looked like she was gonna pop any day now."

Mark had been the godfather of meticulous planning—carrying on a multitude of affairs, building a cabin in no-man's-land, and fathering a secret child. How the paths of his lies never converged, Jared might never know. "I know I've heard the name Lanie before."

Halley swallowed and picked at the chicken. "Remember the tragic roller coaster accident several years back?"

How could he forget? Even after therapy, counseling, and at one point, medication, Mark never fully recovered. "The seventeen-year-old girl who was killed was named Lanie."

"Yep. The best I can figure is naming the baby Lanie was Mark's way of paying tribute to her."

Jared sighed and rubbed his face. A faint memory squeezed to the front of the line. "Didn't she have a brother too?" He'd gone to the hearing and distinctly remembered a young man taking the stand to testify.

She tilted her head to the ceiling and clicked her tongue. "Yeah. Poor kid was there when the accident took place that night, and he saw everything. I always wondered what happened to him. What was his name?"

Jared's mouth went dry. "Bo…"

"Right. But his full name was Boden, I think. Boden Frazer."

Jared's knuckles went white against the steering wheel. "Yeah. Funny thing…that's my partner's name. But it could be a coincidence, though, right? Two people having the same name isn't impossible."

"No. Not impossible." Halley pinched and tugged at the spandex on her leggings. "But I'd say improbable. How many people do you know with the name Boden? There are tons of Bo's in the world, but I can count with one finger the number of Bodens I've heard of."

Point taken.

His own partner. Jared's ability to put two and two together was usually enviable, yet he'd never connected the dots between Bo and Mark. To make matters worse, Bo hadn't even attempted to hide his identity, and Jared still didn't catch on. He failed at being a friend, he failed at being a son, and now he was failing at being a cop—the only thing he had left.

Maybe Jared had ignored the reality. Of course, Bo looked nothing like he had seven years ago. He'd put on weight and had grown a solid foot since then. He certainly didn't resemble the scared young teen who'd watched his sister die.

One way or the other, he needed to have a sit-down discussion with his partner.

"Jared?"

He glanced at Halley, realizing where he was. They'd been driving for miles, but he had no recollection of getting there. The two solid oaks hugged his car between them, and he put the car in park. "What's up, Hal?"

"Do you think Bo had anything to do with Mark's death?"

"Honestly, at this point, I don't know. I don't know who to trust or what to believe. I mean, Jesus, I thought I knew everything there was to know about Mark, but clearly, I didn't know much about him at all. This cabin didn't even exist to me until yesterday. The real kicker is how well he hid these multiple lives." He shrugged. "I'm barely sliding through the intersection of one life."

Halley leaned over and turned his head. "Mark loved you, Jared. And I am so sorry. I never stopped to think about how difficult this all must be for you. Unfortunately, some people know how to lie. They know how to compartmentalize."

Jared tugged her hand off his face. "You don't have to take care of me. I can do that on my own."

"You don't always have to be the lone wolf, ya know. We *are* in this together now, whether you like it or not. Now, what're we going to do about Bo?"

Jared chuckled. "*We* are not going to do anything. You need to get out here and walk back to the cabin the rest of the way. I have some things I need to take care of in town. And don't worry about Bo. If he's involved, I'll find out. But something tells me there's more to this than either of us knows."

Heat slid through his body and warmed his core as Halley placed a light kiss on his lips.

"I know you will." She smiled and caressed his cheek. She climbed out of the car, then turned and ducked her head back in. "I was thinking. Suzanne was wearing maroon scrubs."

Oh, Lord. Wherever this was going didn't sound good. This entire situation was wrong—looked wrong, felt wrong, and worst of all, the investigation was clouded in misdirection, almost as if someone was pulling the old *look over there while I do this over here* trick. "Okay, and?"

"Well, if she was wearing scrubs, then she probably works at Charlotte General. And the pay phone is only a couple blocks from there. If we knew someone who worked there…" A sneaky grin vined up her cheeks. "You know, like Maggie, maybe?"

Jared shook his head and glared. "Nope. No, no, and no. I'm not dragging Mags into this mess. She's got enough on her plate right now, and this is Mark's disaster, not hers."

"All you have to do is ask her if she works with anyone named Suzanne. She doesn't need to know any more information. Maybe we could even get the last name if Maggie knows her."

Halley had a point. Why was she always pointing out the leads he should've been following? He was ignoring every piece of evidence tossed in his lap. The reality was that Mark had made his bed, and Jared's job was to figure out who made him lie in it.

Maggie knew everyone who worked at the hospital. If Suzanne worked there, Maggie would be able to tell him her shift times and her department. They had to start somewhere. He growled. "Fine. I'll talk to her about Suzanne, but I don't like this. Not one bit." He handed her the picked-apart chicken and the bag of medicine and water. "If I'm not back by midnight, use Mark's phone to call me."

Halley eyed the ground and kicked the dirt. "Um, about that."

"Where's the phone, Halley?"

"I kinda dropped it in the river…accidentally on purpose."

Never in his life had he met a woman who tested his boundaries like Halley. One minute he had an overwhelming urge to strangle her, and the next, he wanted to take her to bed and satisfy every need that

Mark had never met. Jared let his head fall back against the seat. "You're killing me slowly, woman. Just go. Get inside and do *not* answer the door for anyone. I have a key and can let myself in when I get back. Got it?"

"Are you mad?"

"Not as mad as I will be if you don't start moving."

He studied her movements—slow, injured, and broken. She was a woman carved from trauma. He didn't know much about Halley's life before Mark, but the small bits she'd spilled filled him with pain. He should've been the one to rescue her...not Mark.

A warm sensation slithered from his throat to below his waistband. Pining for his dead best friend's wife earned him a one-way ticket straight to hell, but turning away from her now wasn't an option. Somewhere along the way, as much as he hated to admit his feelings, he'd fallen for her.

Jared snorted. Pricker bushes scraped against the back bumper when he turned his car around. His life had turned into one of those insane reality television shows where nobody knows who the father is, and everyone is cheating.

After he ran home for supplies, he'd find Bo so they could have a little chat.

****

"Hi, Suzanne."

The young woman held her belly and breathed deep, releasing slowly after a few seconds. "What do you want? Haven't you done enough?"

"I don't know what you're talking about. I just heard you were in labor and wanted to come over and check on you and the baby. Is that such a terrible thing?" The fluorescent hospital lights cast a shadow over her face. Suzanne had been the tipping point in her relationship with Mark. She could deal with the infidelities, the empty promises, and the lies. But, to father a child with a woman who wasn't her was unacceptable—unforgivable.

She'd always dreamed of being a mother—to feel unconditional love from someone for once in her life. Her husband had left her because she wasn't ready for motherhood, but life fell into place when she reconnected with Mark. He was supposed to save her, to take her away from the madness. Then, she would make him a father—something he'd longed to be. After Suzanne had the baby, she'd finally get her chance. She'd be a mother without Mark, without any man. "I simply took care of a problem—a problem both of us shared. I thought you'd be happy."

Suzanne cried out and clenched her teeth. "You killed Mark! You murdered the father of my child! We were going to raise this baby together."

She placed a hand over Suzanne's mouth. "If you don't keep your voice down, I'll do the same to you. Are we clear? Mark was scum. He deserved to die, and you're dumber than I thought if you honestly believed he was going to leave his perfect life for you, honey."

"I should've turned you in. I should've told the cops about you weeks ago, you crazy bitch. I saw you take those sedatives out of the supply cabinet, and I overheard you talking to someone on the phone about Mark last week. As soon as I have this baby, I'm going to—"

"What?" She ran a damp cloth across Suzanne's forehead as the needle on the fetal monitor jumped.

"You're gonna tell on me? Nobody likes a tattletale, sweetheart. Besides, you have no proof of anything." She dipped the cloth into a pale-pink bucket and wrung out the excess water. "With my guy on the inside, it'll be your word against mine."

The needle jumped again.

"Shh. Shh. Just relax. None of that matters now anyway. Your pain will all be over soon. You'll have this baby, leave town, and I'll raise her as my own because that's just the kind of person I am."

"You're a monster," Suzanne screamed. "You won't get away with this. I won't let you."

Doctor Wilton walked in wearing white scrubs and blue gloves. "Everything all right in here, Maggie?"

Maggie smiled down at the young, frightened woman, and she almost found an ounce of pity somewhere deep down inside...almost. Suzanne was stunning. She didn't have to look hard to see why Mark had fallen into her arms—beauty, smarts, and a body worth killing for. At least, she did before she got pregnant. "Everything is fine, right, Suzanne? I just wanted to check on her when I'd heard the good news." She winked in Suzanne's direction. "But I think this baby is ready to make an appearance."

Doctor Wilton pulled the sheet back, and Suzanne gripped the bed rails when he checked her dilation. "Ten centimeters, Suzanne." He looked up at Maggie. "My regular nurse is out sick today. Would you be able to assist?"

"I'd love to."

Chapter Eight

What the hell was she supposed to do now?

Halley had officially reached the rock-bottom pits of love. But loving Jared was a full circle away from loving Mark. Sure, Jared treated her like a nuisance at times, but he never treated her like a material object. Of course, she couldn't place all the blame on Mark for the nature of their relationship. She'd hidden from the truth, too scared to see what was happening right under her nose.

For ten long years, she'd fallen back, molded herself into the woman and wife Mark had wanted. And the truth was, she and Mark had used each other. Admitting defeat was the easy part. But figuring out why she went along with the charade for so long? Not as simple.

After her parents died, she'd drifted in and out of fifteen foster homes. She survived holidays with people she barely knew and a few rare beatings from those who were only after the extra money. Some of them graciously treated her like a family member, but she got used to just being another number and another mouth to feed. Lost in the limbo of the system, she counted down the days until she turned eighteen so she could leave that world behind

After enrolling in a local college, she found a job as a waitress and rented an old run-down apartment within walking distance of the restaurant. What she had wasn't much, but it was hers, and she didn't have to share the success or the failures with anyone.

One week after gaining her freedom, she met Mark at a carnival just outside of town. The memory flashed through her brain like a strobe light. The past crept up on her present with fierce vengeance.

"Leave me alone," Halley had growled through gritted teeth. The same two boys had been following her around all night, and frankly, her nerves were beginning to wear thin. The line for the brand-new roller coaster curved around the grassy landing, and at this rate, she might get her chance to ride—tomorrow.

The older boy behind her flicked the back of her hair. "Very nice," he said, sporting an arrogant grin. "If you would just tell me your name, I'd leave you alone."

She turned, holding him hostage with her most unwelcoming glare. She had to think fast. A fake boyfriend ought to get them off her case. "My name is none of your business, so I suggest you leave me alone before I call my boyfriend over here to kick your ass."

Both boys snorted. "What boyfriend? I've been watching your ass all night, and I haven't seen one guy claim you."

Enough was enough. Halley ducked under the divider to enter the overpopulated carnival grounds. Something warm and hotter than a funnel cake fresh from the fryer caught her as she tripped over a rogue cord. The eyes she met were bluer than the cloudless sky.

Halley hurriedly stood and reached for his hand. "Uh, hi, babe. I've been waiting for you to get here so we could ride together." She glanced toward the two boys staring intently at her and back at this unknown, hopefully, knight in shining armor.

"Yeah, right." The older boy howled. "He's not your boyfriend. You're making the whole thing up, so I'll leave you alone."

Suddenly the man placed one hand on the back of her neck while allowing the other to travel down the small of her back. Before she knew what was happening, he dipped her and placed a heart-stopping, senses-melting kiss on her unsuspecting lips.

She stood there, stunned, as he walked to the divider. "What's your name, boy?"

"Um, it's uh, Jimmy."

"Nice to meet you, Jimmy," he said, holding out a hand. "You wouldn't have been giving my woman a hard time now, would you?"

The man motioned for Jimmy to come closer. He whispered something in the boy's ear, and the youngster's eyes grew to the size of a baseball before the man regained his place at her side.

As they turned to walk away, Halley's curiosity took over. "What did you say to him?"

"It doesn't matter." When they were out of sight, the handsome stranger pulled her hand to his lips and pressed a soft, lingering kiss upon her knuckles. "What does matter, though, is that I don't know my future wife's name."

Her hand fell limply. "Future wife?"

"That's right. I'm not the only one who felt on fire after that kiss. Tell me I'm wrong."

She couldn't because he wasn't. "Halley. M-my name is Halley."

He placed a hand on both sides of her face,

bringing her closer to his own. When his lips touched hers, a spark let loose between them, and there was no stopping the flame from burning out of control. When Halley parted her lips, inviting him to take her deeper down the dark tunnel of desire, he accepted.

Her eyes remained closed as he whispered in her ear, "I'm Mark. Let's go get some loaded fries."

****

The memory tripped her. After the last storm, a gigantic root had ripped from the soil, and it swallowed her foot.

Chicken and pills sailed through the air, crashing to the ground just out of her reach.

Halley grappled with the root until her foot came free. She rose to her knees on the forest floor. Dirt, moss, and leaves covered her clothing. Not the first time she'd been suffocated by the earth, and if history continued to repeat, it wouldn't be the last. As she brushed herself off, the rage inside of her came to a bulging head. What was the point of getting up? So life could knock her right back down again?

"Are you happy now, Mark? Is this what you wanted?" she screamed into the still air. "How could you do this to me after everything we went through together?" Even though her questions faded away unanswered, a shot of hidden strength emerged.

He'd offered her something she hadn't had in a long time...security. But safety came at a price—a price she paid for a long time, and one she could no longer afford. When he asked her to drop out of college and take care of their home, she did. When he demanded she stay thin, she dieted and kept her weight down. Halley went above and beyond to meet his requests. In return, she got a mediocre marriage and a false sense of love.

Living in his shadow kept her from finding the real Halley and stopped her from pursuing what she truly wanted in life.

Confronting Mark for the world he'd sucked her into would never be in the cards for her.

She'd never have the opportunity to pack her bags and leave him for cheating, and she'd never get the chance to realize she could do better than the life she'd been living with Mark. And last but not least, throwing her wedding ring in his face for breaking their vows would never come to be.

This was her chance to cut the final tie.

"It's over, Mark," she whispered to the ground. "I can't live like this anymore. It's a lie. It's always been a lie, but now it's time to tell the truth. I don't love you, and I'm not sure I ever really did. You gave me a roof over my head, but you took my spirit as payment. I forgive you, but mostly I forgive myself for allowing the game to go on as long as it did. And finally, *we*, if ever such a concept existed, *are done*."

The golden band encircling her ring finger shimmered in the sunlight. Halley slipped the thin ring off and peered through the circular space that used to symbolize the life she shared with a man who, at one point, possibly loved her. Now the ring meant nothing, and the vows living within the precious metal belonged in the ground with her husband.

Halley whipped the ring through the air, and a soft whistle echoed as it spun. She didn't watch the landing. Wherever the broken promises fell was where they'd rest for eternity.

Her splinted arm pulsated as she retrieved the chicken and little white pills she'd desperately need within the next hour. The cabin looked bigger now as she crested the hill, leaving her shrinking life in the dirt behind her.

****

Bo held off telling Captain Maxwell about the tox screening and missing evidence. If a snake was clogging up the pipes, he couldn't be sure who to trust. He folded the results into a tiny square and inserted the sheet of paper into his shirt pocket, glancing in every direction.

Steve had left for Mexico only hours ago and agreed to keep quiet for the time being.

Bo shook his head and waltzed to the computer centered in the hallway, trailed by the department screw-up, Cordini. Craning his neck, he looked back at the balding, bushy-eyebrowed mama's boy. "What's up, Cordini?"

Cordini shrugged his shoulders. "Nothin'. I clock out in a couple of hours and was gonna head over to Dante's for a brew. You wanna meet up later? We can have a few beers and get a few numbers." He jabbed Bo annoyingly in the ribs.

"Uh, thanks for the offer, but I'm actually clocking out now and have a few errands to run. Plus, I have an early morning ahead of me."

"No, that's okay. I understand. Maybe some other time." He scratched his forearm. "Did Detective Arnold find you?"

"Was he looking?"

"Yeah. He wanted to talk about the Martin case."

Bo nodded. "Great. Thanks. I'll see if I can't find

him on my way out." He couldn't stand Cordini, but he felt sorry for him at the same time. The man caught more shit than a manure spreader. His uncle, the mayor, was the only reason he got a job in the department. Cordini couldn't pass his police academy training, so nepotism won out.

It might not have been so bad if the department hadn't given him a spot already spoken for by someone who *passed all their training*.

After Cordini turned the corner, Bo headed down the hallway and poked his head into the office Detective Arnold was using while he was in town.

The lights were on, but nobody was home. The computer screen lit up, and the blue light bounced off the window.

He looked around and made sure no one was coming before he walked around the desk.

His name, next to a photo of him from the hearing, jumped off the screen at him.

Detective Arnold knew. But exactly what information he'd obtained was still a mystery. After all, the case was public record, and a simple background search would bring up every shred of info on the incident. The only difference was that the past never mattered to anyone else until now.

When Mark was murdered, Bo's name was bound to be found eventually, and the motive was damning.

He left Detective Arnold's office and made a beeline straight for his truck. His phone buzzed rapidly in his pocket, and he squinted at the screen, not recognizing the number. "Hello?" he whispered from the sidewalk outside the station.

"Officer Frazer. It's so nice to talk to you again.

Your uniform could use a good ironing, if I do say so myself. The wrinkles don't look very professional."

Bo searched the parking lot, surveying every inch of land nearby. "What the hell do you want?"

"I already told you what I wanted. I told you to keep your nose out of my plot, but you just can't leave well enough alone, can you? If your captain finds out about your little blackmailing scheme, you'll lose your badge. I've already taken care of one little badger who dug up your secret, so I suggest if you want to stay where you're at, you'll keep your mouth shut and go back to arresting drunks at the local dive."

Taken care of one badger? What did they mean by that?

"What's the matter?" Bo taunted. "You afraid I might actually figure you out? You know what they say, 'If you can't do time, then don't do the crime.' " He ended the call, hopped into the truck, and turned the key, exhaling as the engine roared to life.

He'd have to be more cautious now. This maniac already willingly killed once and seemed to enjoy the thrill. They probably wouldn't require much prodding to make them snap again—especially if they felt no remorse the first time around. A shiver ran down his spine, and he pushed a hand through his hair. How someone could end a life was beyond his understanding. Nobody had a right to play God; yet every day, murders, kidnappings, and hostage situations happened in their own backyard.

His mind drifted back to the night of the accident.

Lights from the rides had flashed around them. Lanie and her boyfriend, Colton, stood in line for hours to ride the *Tornado Tanker*—the tallest roller coaster to grace the Blackstone County Fair. The town took full advantage of their newest attraction, advertising the ride for months. Every kid in his class was in line behind them.

The last words he said to his sister played on repeat.

"Come on, Bo. You can sit in the seat between Colton and me."

"Nah. Not right now," Bo said, holding his stomach. "I ate too many ribbon fries. I don't want to throw up all over the crowd. I'd never live it down."

"Don't be such a wimp." Colton ruffled Bo's hair and wrapped his arm around Lanie's waist."

"I'm not a wimp. I just ate too much food."

"Lay off, Colton." Lanie playfully smacked Colton's chest. "If Bo doesn't want to ride, he doesn't have to." Her violet eyes sparkled in the multi-colored, flashing carnival lights as she smiled. "Just don't run off. Mom and Dad said if I lose you, I'm grounded." She winked at him before she hopped onto the platform and strapped herself into the ride.

A man with a dragon tattoo winding up his leg walked around and tugged on the lap bars to ensure they were secure.

Bo stared in amazement as the coaster spewed steam while chugging up the first hill.

They made their way through the first upside-down loop without any issues, but Colton was pressing down on Lanie's lap bar, screaming something from his seat.

Bo's stomach turned as he studied the fearful expression on Lanie's face when they took the final loop.

The bar flew up, and Lanie tumbled like a rag doll

from her seat.

Lanie held on for a second before falling, her body smashing onto two levels of tracks on the way down.

A chain-link fence had been the only thing separating him from his sister's mangled body.

Bo smacked himself in the face, forcing the memory away. He whipped his truck into the Quick Stop parking lot while he fought to slow his breathing. Nightmares woke him night after night, images of Lanie's face lingering in his mind long after he awakened.

The judge ruled the incident an accidental death due to mechanical failure.

Bo read and re-read the reports repeatedly over the years, tirelessly sifting through every piece of information available.

Mark knew something wasn't right, but he'd signed off anyway.

That wasn't an accident or mechanical failure. That was an engineer who was too lazy to do his job—an engineer who didn't want to spend the extra time replacing the fucking locking mechanism.

Bo scrolled through his contacts and tapped on Jared's name. Detective Arnold was closing in. Bo hadn't killed Mark, but he'd be questioned regardless, and withholding information made him look guilty.

Honestly, he was shocked Captain Maxwell hadn't called him with a suspension notification yet…assuming the detective had shed light on his connection to Mark.

It was time to come clean about everything.

Chapter Nine

Jared dragged his duffel bag from beneath the full-sized bed. Dust clogged his nostrils as an army of dust bunnies rose like a puff of smoke.

A-choo, a-choo. Jesus. Time had gotten away from him. Another round of sneezing ensued.

Vibrations and ringing sounded in his pocket. Bo's number scrolled across the screen, and Jared's shoulders tensed. He'd ruminated over and over in the car about what he'd say when he got the chance to talk to his partner. Should he be straight up, or would it be better if he beat around the bush and tried to coax the truth out of the man slowly?

Either way, the conversation was bound to be uncomfortable, and Jared didn't do well with awkward. Other people's personal lives made him queasy. The more you knew about a person, the more intimate your involvement became. He had a small circle, and he'd like to keep things that way. Although, had he probed more into Mark's goings-on, maybe his friend would still be alive.

"Hey, Bo. Long time no talk. Had any breaks in the case?" The breaths on the other end of the phone were heavy like Bo had just run a marathon. "You all right? Sounds like you're out of breath."

Bo was only twenty-two and built like a linebacker. He topped out at six foot three and worked out every day. So why would someone in top physical condition be trying so hard to breathe?

"Jared, I don't have a lot of time, so listen up. Remember when Halley Martin said she couldn't remember anything after the wine?"

"You mean the wine we couldn't find?"

"Mm-hmm. Well, I asked Steve to run a tox screen on Mark."

"Why? Did the captain or Arnie order one?"

"Uh, no. They don't know I asked Steve to do that." Bo's breath quickened. "The toxicology report showed high levels of sedatives in his system."

Jared's mind spun. Halley was telling the truth. But who removed the evidence before he and Bo showed up at the scene? "Are you sure?" He unzipped the duffel bag. "I don't understand. Why would you go behind the captain's back and have Steve do that for you? If they find out, you'll be in deep shit for not following protocol."

"I'm positive. And I don't care about protocol right now. We also found a hair that didn't belong to the victim, but the strand disappeared before we could run it through the system. I think we have a rat."

"Is that why you've been sneaking around?"

Bo sighed. "You're the only one I can trust. This goes deeper than either of us. If someone on the force is behind Mark's death, they're watching our every move. Knowing Mark had been sedated could give us an edge if they don't know that we know. From what Steve told me, it's a common drug—found in any hospital and easily accessible on the streets."

Hospital? Maybe Suzanne was responsible. The person he tackled in the kitchen wasn't pregnant, but she could've easily hired a hit. At least he had a lead worth checking out.

"Okay. Okay. Thanks for letting me know. Here's what I want you to do." Jared still had to get him alone. Just because he was voluntarily dishing out information didn't mean he was innocent. "Are you listening?"

"Yeah. I'm listening."

"Can you meet me at Dante's Bar in one hour? We can go over all this then. In the meantime, call Arnie and have him meet us at Dante's in one hour. Can you do that?" Bo's old pickup roared to life in the background.

"Sure. Are you sure we can trust him?"

"No. But we need more manpower, and I think he's our best bet at luring out the snake in our garden."

"Okay. And Jared?"

"Yeah?"

"Every officer on the force is looking for Mark's wife. So make sure you're watching your back and be careful."

The screen went black, and Jared stuffed the phone into his back pocket. Did Bo know he'd been helping Halley?

Nausea and anxiety took over as Jared threw some extra clothes and toiletries in and zipped up the duffel bag with one sweeping motion. He tossed the strap over his shoulder and ran out the door. Gravel crunched under his feet, and he opened the trunk, shoving the bag into the only clean corner.

"What do you think you're doing?"

He jumped, the heavy trunk lid connecting with the top of his scalp. "Damn," he griped, turning to find Maggie.

She uncovered her mouth and laughed. "I'm so sorry, Jared. I didn't mean to scare you." Maggie's stomach bounced, and a ray of light from the falling sun lit her hair on fire.

A goose egg had already started to form. "Glad to see you find my pain so amusing."

"Oh, lighten up," she scolded. "I was just going to tease you about your duffel bag. I haven't seen that dirty old thing since you started dating Anita Weltzer a few years back."

"Good ole Mags. Do you have to remember every last one of my failed relationships?"

"No—" She chuckled. "—just the crazy ones."

Maggie was far from wrong about Anita. Anita Weltzer was one blow away from having a nervous breakdown. Someone wound tighter than a watch was bound to bust a gear at some point.

Jared honestly worried she might burst into flames one day, like spontaneous human combustion.

After a failed attempt at bullying him into marriage, she threw a plate with lilies painted around the edge at his head.

Luckily, she missed, and he was able to get the hell out before he had to play dodgeball with the entire china cabinet.

Maggie grinned. "I know that look. Memory lane can be quite the fickle bitch when she wants to be."

"No disagreement here." Jared held his hands up in surrender. With Suzanne fresh on his mind, he shoved his hands into his pockets and went all in. No better time than the present. And since Maggie was already standing in his driveway, she spared him having to make an extra call. "Can I ask you something, Mags?"

"Sure. You know you can always ask me anything."

"Do you work with anyone named Suzanne?"

Maggie squeezed her hips, squinting up at the few stars in the sky. "Suzanne, Suzanne. Oh, do you mean Suzanne Akers?"

Jared shrugged. "About five foot four, your build, with long brown hair down to the middle of her back…pregnant."

"That would be her." Maggie beamed. "I heard she was dating some married guy who wouldn't leave his wife."

Yeah. Some married guy named Mark. Hopefully, with enough prodding, she'd give him more.

"You guys talked about that kind of stuff?"

"Not a whole lot. I mean, every once in a while, we had lunch together, but we weren't super close or anything."

"Did she happen to say anything else?"

Maggie displaced the gravel with the toe of her shoe. "Just that she threatened to tell his wife about the baby a few days ago. Supposedly he'd ghosted her afterward. I heard from Carol in maternity that she went into labor right after coming back from her lunch today. Crazy." Her eyes widened. "Is she in some kind of trouble? Does this have anything to do with Mark's death?"

"Look, the less you know, the better. You don't need to be involved in this mess, and I don't want you to get caught up in it by default." He closed the trunk lid.

Jared leaned over and kissed her forehead, breathing in her coconut-scented shampoo. Maybe in another life, he could have wanted more from her, but she was never interested in him, and he let the resentment dissipate a long time ago. Her heart always belonged to someone else.

"Well then, can you at least tell me who the girl is?" Maggie eyed him suspiciously.

"Suzanne? I thought I told you not to worry about her."

"No, Jared. The girl you're seeing," She pointed to the trunk. "You only bring your ratty old bag out when you start seeing someone new."

The back of his neck was going raw from rubbing and tugging at it all the time. "It's still new, Mags. I don't want to jinx anything." More like, he didn't want people thinking he was some kind of jackass for moving in on his dead friend's wife. There might not even be anything to tell. He still wasn't sure how or if he should pursue his feeling for Halley. Mark might've had more hidden sins than the average person, but Jared now had a set of his own, and they weren't likely to be forgiven anytime soon.

Maggie nodded, "I understand. When you're ready to fill me in, you know where to find me." She wrapped her arms tightly around his neck and pecked him on the cheek. As she started across the street, she turned. "Oh, and if you get a chance, ask her if she has a brother. Maybe we could double."

Jared laughed and waved, moving toward the driver's side door. "I'll keep you posted."

He started the car and checked his watch. Dante's Bar was on the other side of town, and he had a forty-five-minute drive ahead of him. Conspiracy theories ran rampant as he pooled all his information. He had one dead guy, at least a dozen mistresses, the possibility that one of them was out for revenge, a mystery person from back at the crime scene, and a probable rat on the inside.

The killer could be one or none. They were all connected somehow, like an intricate web. All the ends would eventually meet, and he wasn't sure he wanted to be around when everything came to a head. But if he didn't figure out who killed Mark soon, Halley would take the fall. The only way he'd let that happen was if he were dead and buried.

****

Jared whipped into the cracked concrete parking lot, and bright floodlights from the overhang blinded him. Using his hand as a visor, he searched around for Bo's truck, spotting the old beater by the far end of the lot, hidden in the shadows.

Jared tucked into a space a few cars down and got out to walk to the truck. The closer he got, the more the floodlights outlined a vague shape of something inside the cab, and exhaust plumed into the cool night air. Bo's headlights were off, and a hand rested on the wheel.

He stopped abruptly and pulled his personal gun, aiming the barrel toward the ground. He crouched low and moved slowly, freezing when he saw a foot near the back tire. Bo might be up to something, and he didn't want to be caught off guard.

Back to the tailgate, Jared slid around the taillights and rounded the back end of Bo's truck.

Arnie was sprawled out on the ground, eyes wide open.

Jared reached down and checked for a pulse, but he

didn't need the stillness to know the detective was dead. Shit.

When he reached the driver's-side door, he reached forward and tapped Bo on the shoulder.

Silence.

Slowly, Jared rose level to his partner and jerked the door handle.

The door opened with an eerie creak.

Bo's massive body tumbled on top of him—limp and motionless—sending Jared flat against the pavement. Rolling his partner onto his back, he checked for a pulse again and blew out a stale breath when a faint heartbeat pounded beneath his fingertips.

Bo's police-issued gun lay in his hand, finger still cradling the trigger. A bullet hole in his chest seeped the familiar crimson Jared had seen far too often over the past few days. He tore off his flannel and placed the fabric over the gunshot wound.

The entire scene looked like a murder-suicide, but Jared wasn't stupid.

Someone had staged the whole thing.

Bo had every intention of meeting with him tonight, so killing himself made no sense. And why Arnie? Was he just collateral damage, or did he know something the rest of them didn't?

Jared dialed dispatch and waited impatiently for the operator to answer.

"9-1-1, what's your emergency?"

"This is Officer Jared Collins. I'm at the far-left corner at Dante's Bar's parking lot, by the side entrance. There are two officers down. I repeat, two officers down. They've both been shot, and only one has a pulse."

Whoever went through the trouble of putting this together had placed the gun in Bo's left hand, obviously unaware that Bo was right-handed. The setup was sloppy and had rookie written all over the mess. Maybe Bo and Arnie were getting too close for comfort—loose ends that needed to be tied up. Whichever way he spun the scenarios, someone out there had a secret, and they were willing to kill to protect it.

Chapter Ten

Where could Jared be? Halley paced aimlessly around the kitchen while her imagination ran through every *what-if* scenario. What if something had happened to him? What if whoever killed Mark got to Jared? She had no way to call—to reach him and make sure that he was okay. If she could kick herself in the ass for ditching her only means of communication, she would.

She shook her head, breaking the chain of thoughts leading her straight down the rabbit hole. Wearing holes in the floor wasn't getting her anywhere, so she grabbed her boots and sat at the table. Before she could slip the first one on, the deadbolt clicked, and the door eased open.

Jared poked his head around the corner.

There was no containing her relief. She threw her arms around his neck and buried her face against his sturdy chest. But he didn't hug her back, and something about his scent smelled off.

"What's the matter? And why do you smell like cleaner or something?" Halley slowly released her arms from his neck and stepped back.

Jared pinched the bridge of his nose and shifted her to the side, making his way to the kitchen table. "Sorry I'm late. I was at the hospital."

Her chest tightened. "The hospital? W-why?"

"It's a long story, Halley. And I've given enough explanations tonight to last me a lifetime. Can we talk about this in the morning? I'll fill you in on all the details the minute I open my eyes, I promise. But I need some time to regroup."

Halley glared at him and planted her hands on her hips. "I've been up all night waiting for you, thinking you might've been killed or mangled in a car wreck…or worse. You have no idea the kind of terrible things that ran through my mind." She turned and moved to the counter, struggling to hop up onto the cold granite with just one arm. "You know what? I don't care why you were late, so just forget I even asked. We were supposed to be partners, but apparently, I was mistaken. You don't owe me any further explanation." She jumped down like a woman on a mission and dashed toward the bedroom.

"Wait just one damned minute, Halley."

Jared's calloused hands were rough and snug as he snagged her upper arm, stopping her an inch from freedom. His tone was different—cold and tired, lacking usual authority. But there was something else in the slight waver of his words…fear. She shook her arm, but his grip didn't loosen. "Let go of me."

"Shut up. Just be quiet for two seconds. Do you have any idea what I've been through tonight? I'm risking quite literally everything by trying to keep your ass out of prison. Do you even care?"

She'd never seen this side of Jared before. His eyes, usually the shade of golden wheat, were dark and angry. The black-and-blue circles underneath gave away his lack of sleep while fury and indignation filled his tone. For a minute, he truly terrified her.

Jared's eyes widened, and he released her arm, regret lining his features as her hand fell. "I-I'm so sorry. I just—Bo's in the hospital. He was shot." He rubbed his forehead. "I know that's no excuse for what just happened, but the incident is why I'm acting like such a jerk."

"What? Are you sure?"

Jared raised a brow and kicked off his boots. "Of course I'm sure. Why do you think I was so late getting here? We set up a time to meet at Dante's, but someone had already shot him when I arrived. I found him in his truck. Well, actually, he more or less tumbled out on top of me when I opened the door." Jared groaned. "On top of Bo's gunshot wound, they killed Arnie."

"Who's Arnie?"

"He was the detective working Mark's case." Jared shrugged. "I'd hoped for some answers tonight, but all I got were more questions and a tile at square one." He fluffed his hair and leaned against the counter. "But the worst part was how the perp staged the entire scene. Can you believe it? They tried to make the whole thing look like Bo killed Arnie and then turned the gun on himself. Bo could get screwed if they believe he's guilty."

"You don't think he did? Even after everything we found out? For all we know, the detective could've been onto him too, and that's why Bo shot the poor guy."

"Trust me on this one. Bo didn't kill Arnie. And as far as finding out any information concerning Bo's past, I'm no closer to knowing the truth than I was before. We never got the chance to talk about the accident or whether he was involved in Mark's death."

Halley deserved the golden-bitch trophy for her earlier performance. Her insecurities had always gotten the best of her. But lately, they'd been more brutal to squelch. Mark's affairs only intensified her feeling of inferiority, and Jared was just the stick who got stuck in the mud made from Mark's mistakes.

Jared wasn't and never would be Mark. But the question remained—could she stop treating him like he was? She settled her hands on Jared's face. "You never did say…did he die?"

Jared fiddled with a loose strand of hair dangling by her ear. "Three hours, Halley. From the time he arrived at the hospital, it took them three hours to remove the bullet from his chest. They said if he survives the night, and there are no complications, then he should make a full recovery."

Halley pulled out a kitchen chair and coaxed him to sit. "So you didn't get anything useful from him?"

Dirty, blond hair brushed against his collar. "Unfortunately, no. But he did tell me over the phone about Mark having high amounts of a sedative in his system at the time of his death. Which means, if there really was wine, someone probably laced the bottle."

"So that's why I couldn't remember anything after I drank some."

"Yeah, but there are still too many knots left untied, though, and I can't figure out how all the pieces fit together."

Halley drummed the table to a beat playing on repeat in her head. "What do you mean?"

"Why would someone go through all this trouble? Okay, yeah, so Mark had a string of affairs with other women. Most people would be looking at the wife in that specific situation. Honestly, trying to pin Mark's murder on you was clever."

She grimaced.

"Sorry." Jared squeezed her hand.

"Just keep going."

"All I'm saying is someone knows more than they're letting on, and now there are two dead bodies and another victim who might not wake up in the morning. I've got a few theories as to why they'd want Bo gone, but nothing concrete. I'm missing something, and it's pissing me off."

Halley sat and fiddled with the hem of her sweater and studied the disheveled man across the table. His hair stuck up in multiple directions, and a blue T-shirt clung to his chest, showing every ripple of muscle. A twinge of guilt cut in line, but she brushed the feeling off.

"There's nothing more we can do right now, Jared. You might as well sleep on your questions until morning, and maybe by then, you'll be able to see things clearer with a rested mind."

"I know," he said. "But I just can't shake this nagging feeling that I'm overlooking something right under my nose."

Halley took his hand, and they stood together. Her breath caught as she rose on her tiptoes to reach his level. Wrapping her hand around the back of his neck, she pulled him toward her. "Like I already said…we can talk about this in the morning."

Her lips parted when she pressed against his mouth, and tingles moved through every inch of her skin. Jared wrapped his arm around the small of her back and pulled her into him, and she moaned as her breasts pressed up against his warm chest.

"This is wrong, Halley. We shouldn't be doing this." Jared trailed his fingers down her injured arm. "Not only are you hurt, but you're not mine to take."

Halley nipped at his bottom lip when he ran his thumb along her inner thigh. This feeling was different from anything she'd ever felt with Mark—passionate and raw, but delicate and honest in the same breath.

Her head fell back, and his lips pressed lightly against her throat before moving along her jawline. The pleasure softened her racing thoughts, but only death could shut them off completely. "I don't belong to anyone. And who's to say what's right or wrong?" She scoffed. "Society? Sure, everyone has the freedom to pass judgment—to create their own ideas of what should be considered morally acceptable..." She tucked her hand up the front of his shirt and traced each perfectly cut muscle. "But unless they've experienced what I have, or they've walked a mile in my shoes, then their opinions are circumstantial at best and, therefore, mean nothing."

A sea of unfulfilled passion and locked-away rage spilled from their heated bodies—bits of confusion and fear spilling with each wave of need.

Halley slid her fingers through his hair and pulled.

Jared growled and ripped open the neck of her nightgown. "I want you, Halley. I've always wanted you. I just didn't know how badly until now."

She cried out when he sucked her exposed nipple into his mouth. She'd remember to return the favor later.

When his tongue slid down her stomach, her limbs trembled, and she no longer cared about anything else, hitting pause on the world around her.

Jared gripped beneath her ass and carried her to the bedroom. He sat her on the edge of the bed and knelt, spreading her legs with a gentle nudge. "Are you sure you want to do this?" he asked, eyes crinkling at the corners.

Halley leaned down and kissed his cheek. "Yes, Jared. I'm sure." For the first time in days, the tug of war between right and wrong, desire and infidelity, converged into one straight line. She put her heart and body into his hands with a clear mind. What he did with her trust now was up to him.

"Lie back." He slid his hand under the hem of her nightgown.

She did as he directed, and her heart pounded as he slipped off her underwear. "What are you doing?"

"Just relax. It's my job to make sure you're taken care of. So let me work."

Cool air brushed against her bare legs, and she jolted when Jared's warm hands dove in between her thighs. Her middle throbbed as he slid his finger up and down against her center.

His breath was hot against her already-heated skin, and she entered a new kind of sexual territory. She gasped when he kissed her somewhere she'd never been kissed before. No man had ever done this to her, and the anticipation made her ache. When his warm, wet tongue circled the right spot, she gripped the mattress. "Oh, holy shit."

He circled and flicked his tongue while he sucked and kissed.

Halley arched her back against the pleasure, and every time she screamed his name, he moved faster.

Jared stopped and stood, melting her with his cocky grin. To be honest, he'd earned every inch of that smile.

Her chest heaved. "I was so close. Why did you stop?"

He pulled her up and freed her from the constricting nightgown remnants she still wore. "Don't worry. I'm not done with you yet." Sweeping her up, he lowered her head onto the pillow and straddled her stomach.

His stubble grazed her breast as he kissed her collarbone, and her body writhed beneath him, wanting more. "Jared, please."

Halley gripped the bottom of his shirt and ripped the thin fabric over his head. She undid the belt on his jeans and released the snap, using her feet to shove his jeans past his penis. The size alone made her gasp. She ran her hands down his hard body and stroked.

He thrust into her hand until he pulled back.

Pinning both wrists above her head, he pressed his lips against hers for one final fiery kiss. "Are you ready?"

Halley nodded. "More than ready."

Jared plunged deep inside her, and for a moment, her mind went blank. She didn't think that was possible. His steady movements brought tears to her eyes as the brink of release closed in on her. She twisted her hips and arched her back to take him deeper—every thrust threatening to send her over the edge.

"I want you to say my name." He looked into her eyes. "Say it."

"Jared," she breathed. "Jared. Don't stop. I'm

close." She dug her nails into his back that was slick with sweat, and she could feel him swell inside her.

With one final thrust, he shoved them both right off the cliff.

Jared dropped his body onto the bed and nuzzled her neck.

Resting her head on his chest, she ran her fingers up and down his stomach to his rock-hard stomach. Their bodies glistened, and her heart pounded in her ears.

"Don't even think about it." Jared panted heavily.

Halley reached over and turned off the lantern. Even in the pitch black, she managed to find his sweet spot with ease. Rising to her knees, Halley swung a leg over Jared's hips and straddled him like the mechanical bull she rode on her twenty-first birthday. She only hoped this time she could hang on for longer than eight seconds.

She lowered her body, and he groaned as she let him enter her again. "Don't worry. I'll do all the work this time."

****

Jared breathed in her scent, thick with sex and honey. They'd made love until the sun burst through the bedroom window, and for the first time in years, his muscles fully relaxed. He brushed the hair away from her neck and snuggled close to the soft spot behind her ear.

So far, he'd been running close to twenty-six hours without sleep, and it didn't seem likely he'd get any today either. "Halley"—he whispered—"you awake?"

"Mm. Kinda." She rolled over, and her hazel eyes lit up like an topaz in the sunlight.

He traced his finger up and down her side in a straight line.

She laughed and shook him off. "Stop. That tickles."

"In a good or bad way?"

"Little bit of both." She chuckled.

Jared couldn't help but stare. Her eyes mesmerized him. How could something so perfect be lying next to him? He didn't deserve this, and he certainly didn't deserve her. His father wasn't right about much, but he was right about one thing. Jared would never make a good husband or father. The genes of his abusive father coursed through his veins, and if he lost control with Halley, he'd never forgive himself.

He smiled. For one night, he had everything. Maybe that would be enough to last the rest of his life.

He threw his legs over the edge of the bed and swiped his jeans off the floor. "I have to get back to the hospital."

"I understand. Don't forget to call Maggie today and ask her about Suzanne."

He had forgotten to fill her in on his conversation with Mags yesterday. "Actually, I talked with her last night when I swung by my place to get clothes and stuff."

Halley sat up and wrapped the tattered sheet around her breasts, although the shredded cloth didn't hide much. "Oh? Well, what did she say? Does she know her?"

"Yes. The woman's name is Suzanne Akers. According to Mags, she went into labor after she got back from lunch yesterday." Jared raised an eyebrow in her direction.

Halley bit her lip and lowered her head. "I didn't mean to upset her. Really, I didn't. I just wanted to know the truth for once. It's all my fault she went into labor."

Wrangling his jeans up over his hips, he walked around the bed and took a seat beside her. "It's not your fault. Who knows what kind of stress she was already under? I'll ask one of the nurses how she's doing today when I see Bo. Will that make you feel better?"

"Bo's on the maternity floor?"

Jared laughed. "They're renovating the recovery unit on the second floor, so they're keeping some of the patients on the maternity floor."

Halley jumped to her feet and wrapped the sheet around her the rest of the way. "Do you think I could go with you? I just want to see the baby for myself. To make sure she's okay."

"No. Not a chance. How many times do we have to go over this? If you get caught, you'll be singing show tunes from a cell." The white T-shirt was a little snug as he tugged at the sleeves, staring her down. Nothing she said could make him cave this time…nothing.

"But I have a plan." Halley held her wrist close to her chest.

"Let me see the damage." He hadn't exactly gone easy on her last night, and he prayed he hadn't injured her more.

"No. My wrist is fine." She clenched her hand and made a fist. "The swelling has gone down a lot since yesterday. At first, I thought I had broken it in the accident, but now I'm thinking it's just a bad sprain."

"Are you sure? Maybe I should just take you to a hospital out of town. They might not recognize you. At least then we can make sure there are no breaks or fractures."

"I said I was fine. We can't risk going to a doctor, even one far away." Halley yawned. "Now. Back to my plan."

Amazing. How could someone so petite have such a large arsenal of plans just rolling around in their head? Jared growled. "I said no."

Halley dropped the sheet.

Stay strong. Just don't even look. She strolled over to him slowly as he averted his eyes to the ceiling. "I'm not looking, and you can't make me."

Halley grabbed his hand and placed his palm on her bare chest. "And I told you that you're not the boss of me. So, Officer Collins, can I go with you?"

Caving wasn't what he had planned, but his eyes went rogue, roaming from the tips of her toes to her wide, shiny eyes. One glance at her svelte body and one touch of her velvet skin woke his buddy below the belt. "You know, I'm pretty sure bribing an officer with your naked body is a felony."

"Only if you charge me."

Jared closed his eyes and let his head fall. He couldn't stop her. If he refused to let her tag along, she'd just find her own way to get there. At least he could keep an eye on her if they went together. "Shit. Fine. What's your plan?"

Halley squeezed him tight and kissed him so hard their teeth touched. "Give me one hour, and I promise you won't even recognize me."

"Okay, but on one condition. If I still, without a doubt, can recognize you, then the plan is scrapped, and you don't leave this cabin. Do we have a deal?" Jared held out his hand. He'd made more deals with this woman in three days than he had in the past ten years with the perps he'd put behind bars. He was shipping her off to law school if they came out of this with a clean slate. She'd make one hell of an attorney.

Halley shook his hand without a word, bouncing all the way to the bathroom.

What did he just get himself into?

****

Maggie had warned him. She explicitly told him to mind his own business. Had Bo bothered to listen, she wouldn't have ordered the hit.

The call came in over her scanner late last night, and she couldn't help but release a sigh filled with relief.

The detective had caught on quickly, putting a wrench in the gears of her carefully crafted plan. After he figured out Bo's connection to Mark, the clock froze. Before long, he'd figure her out too. Too much history existed between her, Mark, and Jared to keep the dust under the rug for long. He had to be disposed of.

Three down, two to go.

She pulled on her scrubs and held the phone in place using her shoulder. "Well? Fill me in. Did you succeed?"

"I, uh...sorta—"

For the love of God. "Why do I get the feeling you failed?"

The man on the other end sniffled. "Please, just listen—"

"Are you crying?"

"What? No. I mean..." He went silent. "Yeah, I

guess I am. And so what? Men are allowed to cry too. I just shot a cop and a detective! This isn't just some slap-on-the-wrist offense. Do you know how long I could go away for?"

Maggie chuckled. "Not as long as you would for killing them, which you did, right?"

"See, that's the thing. Bo didn't exactly die."

She bit down on her pillow, stifling a scream, and punched the spring-loaded mattress. "What do you mean? He's either dead or alive, which is it?"

The man sighed. "He's alive. I heard Jared call dispatch through the cellar doors. Then I had to sneak out, walk half a mile to my car, go back to the crime scene, and take a statement. Bo is at Mercy General now. The captain said he's expected to recover if there aren't any complications."

"You can't do anything right, can you? I knew you were worthless." She ignored the sobbing coming through the phone. "Stop blubbering! Did you at least manage to kill the detective and get rid of you-know-who?"

"Yeah. That Suzanne lady is floatin' down Coleson River as we speak, and Detective Arnold was DOA." He sniffled again. "Won't be long before she either washes up on the rocks or gets picked up by a fishing boat."

"You didn't shoot her, though, right? I want her wounds to be exactly like Mark's. They need to believe Halley struck again. Shooting Bo and the detective was good—makes the killings seem unconnected. And you made it look like Bo was the one who shot Detective Arnold, didn't you?"

"Don't worry. I did what you said."

"At least you did one thing right," Maggie snarked. "I'm heading in to work. I'll finish off Bo before the end of the night." She grabbed her keys from the nightstand and walked out the door, hanging up before he could say anything else.

She sucked in a deep breath, closing her eyes to heighten the smell of leaves and fresh-cut grass. Her father always cut the grass before November snow came. Coming back home was the biggest mistake of her life, next to marrying her sleazeball ex-husband, Robert. If she'd stayed in California, none of this would be happening. Of course, with thousands of dollars in credit-card debt, thanks to his drug addiction, she'd have been living in a box, begging for money, instead of an actual home with a roof and running water.

Everybody cautioned her. The whole town knew what a loser he was, yet young love prevailed—well, for ten years, anyway. Her parents welcomed her home with open arms and a novel's worth of I-told-you-so's.

The night she ran into Mark at the liquor store sealed her fate… and his.

All she needed was a little vodka to numb the pain and embarrassment of a failed marriage that so graciously launched her into a nagging identity crisis. But what she got was an affair she wasn't expecting with a man who stole her heart. The affair started with the intention of comfort—to fulfill an itch she couldn't scratch on her own. But good old Mark, the suave, professional, sweet talker, schmoozed her out of her clothes and sanity like a used-car salesman selling lemons to morons.

Who could've known things would get this far? Mark brought out the dark she'd been suffocating all those years. The battle between good and evil consistently caused tiny tears in her conscience—her mind a constant war zone. But Mark tipped the scales, stealing the last bit of light she had left.

Maggie started the car and cranked up the heat, watching the fog recede down her windshield. Pulling the morphine from her pocket, she tossed the vial gently in the air, gripping the thin glass fast and hard as it landed in the palm of her hand. A full syringe of this in Bo's IV, and then she'd be down to one. She just might get away with this yet.

Chapter Eleven

Bleach...no. Disinfectant...nope. "Aha!" Halley squealed, excited to finally find what she'd been searching for. She'd trashed the area under her bathroom sink, but as long as this worked, the mess would be well worth it. The lightening agent was sitting right in plain sight. She'd bought the box a couple of years back when she had the fleeting thought that blonde might be her color...fleeting being the operative word. Had the bottle been a snake, she'd have bite marks.

Fifteen years ago was the last time she'd tried to screw with her hair color, when she was trapped in one of her earliest foster homes. Two other girls shared the house with her. Together they swiped a few bucks from their foster mom's purse and purchased some lightener from the nearest pharmacy.

The bottle was a hell of a lot cheaper than a real bleaching kit and easier to hide.

Back then, all the popular girls were changing their hair—trading in their dark locks for platinum blonde.

Halley craved to fit in, to be anything other than an outcast or a reject. What kid wants to be known as the orphan—the abandoned girl whose parents died? Instead of wallowing, she had sectioned her hair, poured the liquid on her scalp, and wrapped her scrunched-up locks in a towel.

Instant regret. Her hair looked like shit, and her foster mom beat the hell out of her for stealing the money. But for a couple of weeks, at least, they noticed her for something other than being a nobody.

Halley followed her deluded teenage self's lead. She saturated her hair and held out for thirty minutes. Her heart skipped a beat when she looked in the mirror, and light hairs poked out from beneath the towel above her ears. Now all she needed was a different body.

But how?

"Halley!" Jared yelled from the kitchen. "Are you almost ready?"

"Just give me thirty more minutes, please!" she hollered back, seizing a pillow from the bed. Her hair could stand to lighten longer, but she still had to cut it, and time was running out.

This will have to do.

Halley unwrapped the towel and chuckled at the ridiculous orangish-blonde mane tumbling down her back.

A strange feeling twisted inside her. She wasn't a teenager anymore, but somehow the woman in the mirror sent her back to that time. Little orphan Halley, just meandering through life with no family, no security, and no one who wanted her.

Straightening her back and shifting her shoulders, she pointed at her own reflection. "I am not a girl. I am a woman. I may not have many people who want me in their lives, but I have one, and that's all that matters." Affirmations worked wonders on the psyche…most of the time.

She slung her hair back, and with one final wrap of the rubber band, her hair dangled in a long, damp ponytail. She placed the tail into a pair of open scissors. The ripping sound of hair fraying between the blades liberated her from the woman she used to be and from the girl she once knew.

Gone was the Halley who moved from home to home, from people who didn't care whether she lived or died. She whispered, "Good-bye," to the Halley who played by the rules. And the Halley whose loyalty had been rewarded with a cheating husband and a possible life sentence no longer existed.

She brushed her hair back and secured one of Mark's old ball caps around her head. Positioning the pillow underneath her shirt and zipping up her sweatshirt, she took one final look in the mirror. *Here goes nothing.*

Halley kept her head down and shuffled to the kitchen, where Jared stood waiting impatiently by the door. "What do you think?" Holding her fake belly, she gave him a runway twirl.

He laughed, shoved his hands deep in his pockets, and strolled toward her like a man on the prowl. "I may be good, but I doubt I'm *that* good." Jared nodded to her pillowed stomach and gave a gentle pat.

"Oh, you're not the father." Halley slapped his hand away. "Didn't your mother ever teach you not to touch a pregnant woman's belly?"

His hands flew up in surrender. "Sorry, ma'am. You just look eerily similar to someone I made love to recently. My mistake. Please forgive me."

Halley shuffled toward the door. "Apology accepted." She turned, laying her best pouty lip on him. "You are kind of cute, though. Maybe we could go out on a date sometime. Would you like that?"

Jared took a quick step back. "Hmm. Seems like a lot to take on all at once. What about the child's father?"

"Absent." Halley smacked him on the arm. "Seriously, though. Does my new look pass inspection?"

"I have to give you credit. I'd never have known your identity had I not watched you walk out of the bedroom. Nice touch with the pillow, by the way." Jared looked at his watch and opened the door. "After you, Miss…"

"Oaks. Laurel Oaks."

Jared's eyebrow peaked. "Laurel Oaks? You went with a new first *and* last name? How much thought did you put into this?"

"Enough. I've always loved the name Laurel, and Oaks was the last name of my final foster family."

"Whatever you say, Miss Oaks." Jared stepped onto the porch and helped her down the steps like a perfect gentleman. "Listen, when we get to the hospital, you need to follow my instructions to the letter. Do you understand?"

Halley nodded. "You do know I'm not a child, right? So you can quit asking me if *I got it* or if *I understand*."

Jared crossed his arms and made a funny face. "I don't do that."

"Yes, you do. Maybe you don't realize what you're doing, but I am not one of your trainees at the academy. I take direction very well, thank you."

"I'm sorry. I guess the words just came out." Jared pulled her ball cap down a little lower. "I just want to make sure I can keep you safe. If anything ever happened to you, I'd never be able to forgive myself. Honestly, I don't know if I'd survive losing you." He tucked a stray piece of hair behind her ears. "I love you, Halley. I love you more than life itself."

Tears welled in her eyes, threatening to spill over. "I love you too. And I didn't mean to make you feel bad. But my entire life has been spent under someone else's thumb, and I never want that for myself again. Got it?" she jeered, elbowing him in the ribs.

Jared moaned and doubled over. "They're still tender, you know."

Halley kissed him on the forehead. "Sorry. Still love me?"

"Do you really have to ask?"

For the first time in her life, she didn't. There was no wonder—no doubt. When he said he loved her, she knew he meant every word.

They walked to the car hand in hand. This plan was crazy. No, actually, this was downright fucking nuts. But it just might be insane enough to work.

****

Stainless-steel elevator doors opened, and Jared stepped inside.

"Hold the doors, please!" Halley yelled from down the hall.

She'd executed her part like a professional. Acting like strangers would stop anyone from pegging them as a pair. The plan was simple—she didn't know him, and he didn't know her.

Jared clutched the closing door as Halley squeezed inside. He gripped her shoulders when the door closed and kissed her until the elevator shifted under his feet. "Remember…stay at least six feet behind me at all times. Look ahead confidently but don't make eye contact with anyone. And, Halley. If anyone recognizes you, don't wait for me." He set the car keys in her hand and closed her fingers around them.

"Don't worry. I'll be fine. I love you."

"I love you too."

The bar above the doors had three numbers. When the elevator stopped on the last floor, they scooched apart as the doors opened, stepping out one at a time. Jared turned to his left. Heat crept into his cheeks. Captain Maxwell stood, phone in hand at the end of the hall.

He didn't look back at her…he couldn't. "Take a right and head toward the nursery." He lowered his tone and kept his head up as he walked forward.

Captain Maxwell noticed Jared seconds later. "Collins. Where have you been? I've been trying to reach you all morning."

"Sorry, sir. My phone died, and I have to get a new charger." He wasn't completely lying. His charger worked fine, but he had nowhere to charge his phone with no electricity in the cabin.

"Well, you're here now. That's what matters."

Jared cleared his throat. "How's Bo?"

Captain Maxwell tucked his phone into his shirt pocket, put his arm around Jared's shoulders, and all but shoved him in the direction of Bo's room.

"The doctor I spoke to a few minutes ago said Bo will make a full recovery, but he'll be off for at least two months, if not more."

"That's good news." Jared shrugged away from the captain's grasp. He needed to play cool. With Bo down for a while, and Arnie gone, being put back on the case

145

was a slim possibility.

Bringing in another big-city detective was the more-likely scenario. Until then, Halley's fate rested in Cordini's hands. A man with goose shit for brains.

"You know, sir, I've been feeling much better. I'd be happy to keep tabs on the case alongside Cordini. I'm sure they'll hand everything over to another detective, but that could take another day or two." So much for stealth mode. "The longer the evidence sits, the faster the trail goes cold. We both know what happens when the leads end, Captain. I need to catch the person who did this to my friend."

They halted in front of Bo's room, and Captain Maxwell's face turned to stone. "I'm not particularly interested in what you'd be happy with. You are not to stick your nose anywhere near the Martin case. And don't think I haven't heard the rumors."

"What rumors?"

"Word around the precinct is that you might have a clue about where our missing suspect is hiding out. Is there any truth to the accusation?"

Jared leaned against the wall. "And who exactly has been saying these things."

"I'm not here to play tattletale, Collins. I have a dead detective and a cop with a bullet hole in his chest. From the looks of the scene, Bo shot Detective Arnold and then turned the gun on himself. I want some answers, and I want them now."

"Come on, Captain. Do you believe Bo would do something so heinous?"

Captain Maxwell hiked up his pants. "You tell me. Detective Arnold was looking for Bo, and Alex in accounting said he saw Bo snooping around Arnie's office right before he clocked out. When we searched Arnie's phone, Bo's number was the last incoming call." He sighed and scratched his balding head. "I want you to tell me exactly what happened last night because another number popped up in his call log about an hour before you dialed dispatch. Wanna take a wild guess as to whose number I'm talking about?"

"No, sir. I can take a hint."

"Good. Then start filling in the blanks.

Jared ran a hand through his hair. "I gave Cordini a statement."

"Oh, I read the statement. Short, sweet, and to the point. I believe the report said, *Fuck off, Stan.* Am I wrong?"

He wasn't. Jared had wholly forgotten about snubbing Cordini at the scene. He was too worried about making sure his partner made it to the hospital—not filling out some stupid form. "I just went to meet Bo for a beer. When I got there, I found Arnie lying on the ground by the back tire of Bo's truck. He didn't have a pulse when I checked him on the scene. When I arrived at the driver's-side door, Bo was slumped over with a gun in his hand." He couldn't leave out the part about Bo being set up. "Listen, Captain. I know my word may not mean much, but I'm positive someone staged the entire scene. The gun was in Bo's left hand."

"And?"

"Well, Bo is right-handed. Why would he shoot Arnie and then shoot himself with the wrong hand?" He shook his head. "I'm sorry I didn't fill out the statement correctly. You can write me up if you have to."

Captain Maxwell studied him. "No. That won't be necessary. Your story matches Frazer's. I just wanted to be sure. Also, when Cordini handed in his report, I questioned the same thing. Now, I'm not saying you're right, but I wouldn't say you're wrong either."

"Wait. Bo's awake?"

"Why don't you see for yourself," the captain said, holding the door open, gesturing Jared into the room. "I need to get back to the station, but this isn't over, Collins. If you know anything about our suspect's whereabouts and you're keeping them to yourself, I'll charge you with a felony. Not only will you lose your job, but you'll get jail time too. So get a charger and answer your damn phone next time I call."

"Yes, sir."

"Oh, and one more thing, Collins. Take a shower. You look like shit."

On that upbeat note, Captain Maxwell disappeared from the doorway, leaving Jared alone with Bo to do what he came there to do—get the truth.

Jared walked around the curtain, listening to the steady beep of the monitor. Bo, his partner and potential psychopath, lay still on the thin mattress, his toes peeking out from under the blanket. Guess they didn't have blankets big enough for a giant in this place.

He sat on the chair beside the bed and poked Bo's leg. When his partner didn't respond, Jared jabbed a bit harder.

"You know I was just shot in the chest, right?" Bo croaked, smacking Jared's hand away from his leg. "What are you trying to do, kill me?"

Jared broke his hardened façade. "Not yet, but keep giving me shit, and I might."

"What are you doing here, Jared?"

This was his moment—his opportunity to get answers. "Listen, I didn't come here to pussyfoot around. I know who you are. Who you really are—"

"You know…I never lied about my identity. My secrets were always out there, but nobody ever looked. That's not my fault."

"No. I suppose it isn't. But people are dying, and I want to know if you had anything to do with Mark's murder."

Bo flopped his head to the side and opened his eyes. "Yes. I did. But not in the way you think."

Jared stood so fast his chair tipped over backward and clanged against the floor. "Son of a bitch, Bo. Or should I call you Boden? How could you? We took an oath to save lives, not take them."

"I didn't take anybody's life—not like your friend took my sister's." Bo coughed and pressed a hand over the large white gauze bandage covering his left pec. "I gave Mark a packet of photos. I'd been tailing him for a while. I told him if he quit working on roller coasters, I wouldn't tell his wife about his *other* interests."

"What happened next?"

"Nothing. Mark said he'd quit after his last job in Colorado. But I swear on my life, I never touched him, and I sure as hell didn't kill him."

Pinching the bridge of his nose, Jared bent to pick up the chair. "You know what happened with Lanie was an accident, Bo. Don't you?"

"Yeah, well, you didn't see her face when she slipped out of the safety bar that your friend signed off on as safe. Maybe if you had, you'd understand. After Lanie died, my mom drank herself to death, and my dad disappeared. I basically raised myself, so spare me your self-righteous indignation."

Jared couldn't begin to imagine Bo's pain, but he'd been down the road of abandonment. Being so young and seeing—living something so traumatic took a mental toll. Had the roles reversed, he might've done the same thing. "Listen, why don't you just tell me about what happened at Dante's? We can start from there and move the pieces as we go."

"All I remember is putting the clip in my gun. As soon as I heard the click, I felt a sharp pain in my chest. Then I blacked out."

"You sure that's all you can remember?"

"I'm sorry, Jared."

A nurse came in just as Jared opened his mouth to speak. "Is everything all right in here? Your voices carried down to the nurse's station."

"Yes, ma'am. I'm sorry if we disturbed anyone. I was just leaving." Jared turned back to Bo. "We'll finish this conversation later. Just get some sleep and recover."

Bo waved him out of the room and turned his head away.

Jared left the room and headed down the long hallway, searching for Halley. He gently pushed on the double doors leading to the nursery and found her face pressed up against a wide glass window, looking at a room filled with six babies.

"Hey, Hal. I'm done here."

"Great! What did Bo have to say? Is he innocent?"

"In a manner of speaking." Jared rubbed the back of his neck. "He said he just gave Mark the pictures along with an ultimatum. To stop putting up roller coasters, or he'd tell you about the affairs."

Turning, she linked her fingers with Jared's. "You don't think he's the killer?"

Jared shook his head. "I believe him. I don't think he's capable of murder. But I do think someone is trying to kill him for knowing too much, which I'm guessing is connected to Mark's affairs somehow." He touched her cheek. "You okay? Did you find Suzanne's baby?"

Halley pointed to a small pink blanket with a tiny bald baby wrapped up inside like a burrito. "She's that one, right there." She sobbed briefly.

Jared's inexperience in relationship territory shone through. He wanted to hold her and console her, to take her pain away. But something told him this was about more than just seeing a cute baby through a window. "Do you want to talk about what's bothering you?" He wrapped an arm around her shoulders and pulled her into his chest.

She lifted her head. "While I was looking at the babies, a nurse came by. I told her I was a friend of Suzanne Akers." The rapid sobs started again.

"Calm down and tell me what happened."

"The nurse told me Suzanne decided to put her baby up for adoption. Jared, the baby is going to grow up in the system, and it's all my fault."

Nothing he said would make her feel any better. She never talked much about her parents or what life was like growing up in foster care, but scars like that ran deep. They might fade with time, but they never healed completely. Holding her there in front of the glass, he kissed the top of her head, and together, they spent the next couple of moments staring at babies.

Chapter Twelve

Bo couldn't look Jared in the eyes. He'd been so focused on ruining Mark's life that he rolled into town blinded by fury and rage, never once taking into consideration the damage he was doing to innocent parties. Halley didn't deserve the dish being served, and now Jared was neck-deep in *his* mess. He pressed a hand to his chest, running his fingers across the glossy patch covering his gunshot wound, remembering the sharp pinch as the bullet entered his skin.

Bo recalled shutting off his truck and seeing a shadow near the dumpsters. As he turned to open the door, a searing pain rolled through his chest. Then he woke up in the hospital, smelling like disinfectant. They must've shot him through his rolled-down window. He didn't see the gun or the coward wielding it, but maybe he deserved this hole. Perhaps this was the payback for what he'd started. Now someone was going out of their way to make him a member of the six-feet-under club, and he was less than enthused about the invitation.

Going down this easy would be an admission of defeat.

Over his dead body.

Bo wrapped his fingers around the thin tubes connected to his arms and pulled up in a swift and precise movement. Rainbow-colored fluids dribbled to the floor. Once he got out of town, he'd call Jared to apologize, and then, if time allowed, he'd confess his sins to the captain. His badge would be worthless, but his conscience would be clear. And wasn't that what everyone yearned for…a clear conscience?

Slowly, he stood, leaning against the wall to steady his swaying body. The blurry hospital bag resting on a chair in the corner came into focus. His clothes were wadded into a ball and soaked with blood, but alternative clothing options weren't exactly raining down upon him. He'd have to go out the same way he came in—bloody and half dead.

After completing the agonizing task of dressing himself, Bo peered out into the hallway towards the nurse's station. The same bitchy nurse who had been forcing broth down his throat for the past five hours checked her watch and stood. When she turned her head in his direction, he ducked back into the room. He poked his head out like a turtle in a shell and sighed. No nurse. The station was empty, and silence filled the floor.

If ever a time existed to make a jail break, it was now.

****

Halley stared out the car window and listened to the radio:

"The murder of a local man, Mark Martin, has shaken the tight-knit community. With the suspect still at large, people are locking their doors for the first time in decades. Two more shootings occurred late last night, leaving one man dead and another seriously injured. Sources say—"

Jared leaned forward and turned the dial. "Oookay. That's about enough."

She glanced at the floor, then back out the window, baby Lanie's face flitting through her mind. She ruminated over her conversation with Suzanne. Calling that pay phone was dumb. Had she kept her big mouth shut, Lanie would have a warm home and a loving mother to fall into—someone who would sing her to sleep and read her stories. She'd have a mother who would try to make her homemade baby food and fail miserably. Lanie deserved a mom like Halley's.

When she looked into Lanie's dark-blue eyes, a sense of kinship invaded her soul. Halley's parents didn't want to leave her, but the uncertainty and feelings of abandonment played a huge part in her insecurities. Even when the past scabbed over, the memories still left their mark.

The road to hell was paved with good intentions, and she held no ill will toward the foster parents who took her in. Some were good, and some were…questionable. There were five good ones for every rotten home, and Lanie was a baby. Everybody wanted a baby. Unfortunately for Halley, nobody wanted a teenage orphan with baggage.

I'll pray for you, kid.

The car stopped between the two massive oaks, and Jared cut the engine. "What's going on inside your head, Halley? Whatever's happening, I want to help."

Halley sighed. "You can't help. Not with this. My heart breaks for Lanie and for the mother who will never get to know what an amazing child she brought into the world."

"Some people don't have the resources or the ability to take care of a child. Did you ever stop to think that this might be the best thing for her?"

"I know. Just forget about it. You wouldn't understand."

Jared grabbed her shoulders and turned her to face him. "You're right. Maybe I don't understand everything you went through, and I can't imagine how hard losing your parents and being bounced around from family to family must have been. And yes, I had a mom. A wonderful, loving mother, but my dad was less than stellar in the parenting department. He beat my mom and me until he just got tired of dealing with us one day. He walked out on our family and never looked back. So don't tell me I don't understand." He gripped her chin. "Your parents wanted you. They didn't leave by choice. My dad would've given me away the minute I was born had my mom not stopped him."

Halley removed his hand from her shoulder and linked her fingers through his. "I didn't mean to upset you. I just—every time I think about my parents, I get so angry, like God cheated me out of love. I mean, what did I do to deserve this life?"

"You didn't do anything, Hal. Neither of us did. Life happens, shit happens, and you can't always stop the bad." He removed the ball cap from her head. "What were they like, your parents? You never talk about them."

Shrugging, she took a deep breath in and held the air in her lungs for a moment, exhaling slowly. "My mom was beautiful. She had short, black hair and emerald eyes. I remember she always smelled like flour. She loved to bake." Halley smiled. "My dad was tall, tough, and never said much except for how much he loved Mom and me. When he wrapped me up for hugs, I knew nothing could get to me. They were amazing."

For years she'd stuffed those memories away, unwilling to feel the hurt she'd locked away. This time though, the memories brought something different. There was no pain, only joy. Her heart burst with happiness and comfort as images of her parents swarmed, buzzing through her mind like a busy bee. Maybe locking the past away wasn't the answer. What if the answer was keeping the memories alive while allowing movement and growth?

She'd allowed herself to stay stationary for too long. But not anymore.

Let go, Halley.

The final tie holding her back disintegrated as she closed her eyes, releasing a final breath. Nothing could keep her from the life she wanted and deserved. Luckily, the next chapter was sitting right beside her.

Halley moved closer to Jared, bumping his chin with her nose. "Have I told you how amazing you are?"

He puffed out his chest and grinned. "No. But thank you for saying so."

Halley swept across the console, placing one knee on each side of Jared's thighs. "Instead of just saying how I feel, how about I show you?"

"Now, this is an idea I can get behind." Jared moved the seat back and pulled a lever on the side, shifting them into a horizontal position.

Without speaking, she removed his shirt and forged a line of kisses down his chest to the button of his jeans.

"Jesus, Halley." He moaned.

She gripped the sliver of fabric and unsnapped the button with a swift tug. "What do you want me to do to you, Jared?"

"Anything you want." His breaths were unsteady as he spoke. "Anything at all."

Halley tugged down his jeans as he lifted his hips, and she brushed her lips against his thigh.

As she gently wrapped her hand around his cock, Jared shuddered. She might not have much experience in the sex field, and this was the first time she'd ever made love in a car, but practice made perfect, right?

Raw passion and desire flew from her fingers as she stroked him hard and steady. This time, he'd be saying her name.

"Holy fuck, Halley."

There it was.

She stopped before he could release. "What else do you want?"

He sat up and opened the car door. "I want you." He slid out of his seat with her still in his arms and rested her back against the tree. He winced. "Damn."

"Are you okay?"

"No. My ribs hurt like hell, and bark isn't very forgiving."

"Do you want to stop?"

Jared grinned. "Even if every bone in my body was broken, I'd still choose you over comfort every time." He squeezed her ass.

How could he make her senses disappear like this yet heighten them at the same time? She was irrational when it came to Jared. But when they made love, she went crazy.

"And I want this." Jared's muscles flexed as he gripped her hips.

Her nipples were hard and ready for his tongue. She moaned as he slid his fingers into her pants and massaged her wet center. Need built with every pass, and her body writhed uncontrollably against his hand.

"Take off your pants. Now," Jared demanded.

Halley tugged at her pants and kicked them to the side, leaning back against the tree trunk, taking in every inch of his naked body.

She didn't want to be dominated. This time, she was in charge, and now nothing stood between her and a shot at ecstasy.

"Is this what you want, Jared?" Halley walked toward him and pushed him into the driver's seat.

"What are you doing?"

"Shh. I have a plan." Halley straddled his legs and lowered herself onto his shaft, letting him fill her insides.

Jared lifted her hips up and down in a steady motion.

Bolts of electricity coursed through every nerve ending each time he entered, and all worries melted into the dirt along with her pants. The only thing that mattered was a simultaneous release. When they fell over the edge, she'd make sure they plummeted together. "Faster, Jared."

He listened, picking up the pace, lifting and dropping her harder and faster. "Halley, I can't hold on." He grabbed onto the wisps of hair she had left.

"Then just let go." Halley dug her nails into his shoulders as he swelled, filling her with love. She pulsated from the pleasure.

They both came in a blurry haze—one she'd treasure and remember for the rest of her life.

Euphoria surged as she rested her head on his chest, still allowing him to savor their connection.

When she felt his muscles loosen, she detached her body from his and crawled back to the passenger seat.

Jared's phone rang while he buttoned his jeans. Thankfully the old phone charger in his car had still worked. "It's the captain."

"Well, aren't you going to answer?"

She only caught half of the short conversation, but the frown on his face made her stomach lurch.

Jared tossed his phone onto the dash. "Will you be all right here by yourself for a while? I have to go." He walked over to her pants and picked them up from the ground, then handed them to her through the window.

"I'll be fine. What's going on?"

Turning the key in the ignition, he brought the car to life. "Suzanne Akers is dead."

****

"Cordini!" Jared yelled from the civilian side of the caution tape.

The middle-aged gorilla stood by the ambulance and glanced in his direction. Black tufts of hair spilled over the collar of his uniform. Too bad they couldn't use the extra body fur to replace what ran away from his scalp. The man's head was emptier than a box of free donuts in the station's break room, which was probably why his hair wouldn't grow—not enough nutrients upstairs to keep the follicles alive.

"Hey, Jared!" Cordini hollered back. "Duck under and check this out."

"Dipstick," he mumbled, lifting the yellow tape over his head, entering a circus run by an incompetent ringleader.

Captain Maxwell made his orders clear as a bell. Jared was not, under any circumstances, to barge back into the investigation and take control. But they were both well aware of Cordini's ability, or lack thereof, to handle the paperwork. More than one perp had been released back to the streets thanks to Cordini's screwups. A new detective was on their way from upstate, but they weren't counting on another body.

"Check over the body, fill out the paperwork, and bring it back to the station." Those were the captain's direct orders, and Jared aimed to follow them. Although, a little inconspicuous prying never hurt anybody. A bit of faux friendliness, and he'd have Cordini singing like a canary.

Cops polluted the area.

Jared twisted and walked toward Cordini, who stood next to a stretcher with a body zipped up in a black bag. He reached over and plucked the clipboard from the man, then skimmed over the empty sheets. "Cordini, why is none of this filled out?"

"Oh, well, I was gonna fill it out later, after I got back to the station."

His voice sent a chill down Jared's spine like nails on a chalkboard, and the urge to punch him in the face became overwhelming. He could attempt to feign surprise, but acting wasn't his forte. "You're supposed to fill this shit out as you go, so you don't miss or forget any of the details. This is why none of our cases hold up in court!"

Cordini snatched the clipboard back and started jotting things down like a madman, giving Jared a perfect opportunity to fish for information.

"So, do we know anything about the victim?"

Cordini scratched his head with the ink side of the pen. "A teenager fishin' off the bank under the bridge saw her floating in the water. We walked the bank and found a wallet with identification in it just a few yards down."

"You got a name and age?" Jared bit his tongue. Flicking the moron between the eyes wouldn't be considered assault, would it? Maybe he didn't need to be so rough on the guy, but he'd seen bugs collaborate more intelligently than this dink.

"Yeah, um…"

"Forget the name," Jared said impatiently, waving his hand in the air. "The captain called me earlier, so I know her name is Suzanne, but I need an age."

"I think her license said twenty-two." Cordini walked over, unzipped the body bag, and pulled the small purple wallet from inside the bag. "Here." He handed it to Jared.

Jared met his gaze and lifted a brow. "You're shitting me, right? Why was this in with the victim instead of an evidence bag?"

"Well, I forgot to bring those."

God made that boy a special kind of stupid.

Jared pulled a small plastic bag from his back pocket and dropped the wallet inside. He always carried a few around with him, just in case. "Can you show me the body?"

"Sure can." Cordini complied, pulling the zipper to the bottom of the bag. "But I gotta warn ya. She looks kinda gross."

What kind of cop used the word gross when describing a dead body? A man with too much job security, that's who.

Parting the bag's sides away from the victim, Jared analyzed the stab wounds. The vertical and horizontal slices covered Suzanne from chest to abdomen—just like Mark's. Jared shook his head, pinched the bag together, and zipped it back up. He'd seen more knife holes in the past week than during all his years on the force combined.

"Remind you of anyone?" Cordini tapped his foot on the concrete and slapped Jared on the back. "I bet the same person who killed your friend killed this lady too. Probably that guy's wife, Holly."

"Her name is Halley, you moron." Jared's patience had left the building. If he didn't get out of there soon, an explosion would ensue, and he might enjoy beating the crap out of Cordini too much to stop.

"Geeze. You don't have to be so testy. I heard from someone down at the station that she disappeared right off the face of the earth. Every time they search for her, they come back empty-handed."

And they always would so long as Jared was involved. He took the clipboard back from Cordini and skimmed over the paperwork. Nobody could read this chicken scratch. "All right, look. You need to rewrite this report because a kindergartener could've done a better job, and I'm going to the hospital to check on Bo. Do you think you can manage for twenty minutes until I get back?" Jared handed the clipboard back to Cordini.

Cordinin reluctantly reached out and shot him a puzzled look. "You didn't hear?"

Good God, what now? "Hear what?"

"Bo left the hospital about an hour ago. Captain Maxwell has been trying to reach him, but nobody can get hold of him" Cordini grinned. "Funny. I would've thought he'd tell his partner he was jumping ship."

"How do you know he left?"

"Called over to see how he was holdin' up, and the nurse lady told me he skipped out. The captain called a few minutes later. Must've had the same idea as me."

A bullet hole to the chest warranted more than a day in the hospital. Warning signals whirred in Jared's brain. Bo was going to run.

He bolted from the crime scene, and Cordini yelled after him. "If you take Lake Street, you'll miss all the after-work traffic."

Jared bounced into his car and took off, leaving the crime scene in his rearview mirror. He hated to concede it, but Cordini was right. Lake Street never did carry much traffic, and according to his calculations, he'd arrive at Bo's apartment in about thirty minutes if he kept up his speed. Hopefully, the man hadn't left town yet.

Chapter Thirteen

Clouds shifted overhead, rolling across the dark gray sky at an accelerated rate. The radio spat out severe storm warnings for later in the evening. Guess Mother Nature wanted to get the party started early.

Pelting rain, jagged lightning, and cranky thunder—Maggie loved them all. The way they did their thing—creating chaos and beauty at the same time—intrigued her, even as a little girl. They were so unpredictable, yet people never stopped trying to figure out their next move. But that's not what really sucked her in. A storm's ability to be cold, calculating, and destructive in ways beyond the mere human imagination was what truly amazed her. Who knew nature could carry such a vivid personality?

Thunder boomed nearby, rattling the windows in her compact car. She pulled off at the barely visible opening between the two guardrails. She leaned back against the headrest as the floodgates in the sky opened, releasing waves of water, coating her windshield.

Maggie let off the brake and dove into the divot, turning the wheel to counteract the slide. She hit the gas as she started up the adjacent hill and barely made the climb to the other side.

Her plans had unraveled practically at every turn, and Bo's untimely escape was the final straw. She couldn't let him get to Jared, but she still had to kill

Halley, get the pictures and the card Bo had on him at all times, and go back for the baby. She picked up her burner phone and called for backup.

"Stan. Can you hear me?"

"Hey, Maggie. Yeah, I can hear ya."

She rolled her eyes. Out of all the officers in Charlotte, she'd picked Stan Cordini for his easily moldable emotions. If he'd ever been with a woman, the encounter was probably by accident or thanks to a buy-here, blow-here doll.

The man had the IQ of a twig and the body of an ape. When evolution hit the rest of the population, it forgot Stan. "How many times have I told you NOT to say my name?" Maggie slammed on her brakes as she crested the final knoll, squeezing between two tall trees. She had arrived—foot traffic only from here on out. "Did you tell Jared about Bo?"

"Yep!" he said proudly. "Snuck the info in there like a pro. Jared thinks the whole station's out lookin' for Bo, but they aren't. I just told him that. You should have a little while before he gets back. He doesn't suspect a thing. Hey, what's that sound?"

"It's raining. Coming down in sheets." Maggie banged her head against the steering wheel. She'd held more titillating conversations with the cactus in her room. "So?"

"So what?"

Did she have to spell it out for him? "Do you know for sure he's with Bo?"

"Oh. Yeah. No worries. I have eyes on them right now. Want me to bring them to you?"

Maggie smiled. Maybe she could salvage some wreckage after all. She'd have to off Stan, of course, but that was no significant loss. "No. Not yet. Give me a call when you have them in the squad car together. I'm waiting for the rain to let up before walking to the cabin. I have some unfinished business to attend to."

She ended the call and sighed. Bo had something she needed. He was injured and wanted out, so as long as he paid up, she'd give him just that. And Halley meant nothing to her—just skin, bone, and blood. When Maggie killed her, the death would just be another notch in her belt.

On the other hand, killing Jared would sting like a bullet wound. After all, they were childhood friends. But shouldn't a true friend be there when one of their own was hurting? He'd never called to check on her after the divorce. He didn't comfort her when she needed a shoulder to cry on, and he didn't hold up his end of the friend bargain.

Maybe if he had, she wouldn't have leaned so hard on Mark. She could've saved herself from the consuming pain, but now she was just numb. Come to think of it…this was all Jared's fault.

As the rain slowed, Maggie meticulously stepped into the last set of muddy tracks, careful not to draw any unnecessary attention to her presence. The sun hadn't completely set, but had long since disappeared behind the veil of storm clouds, and night, for all intents and purposes, had fallen.

A deep-yellow hue flickered through the curtainless window, and Maggie ducked low behind a pile of brush when Halley's outline darted past the filthy glass. She swallowed the unmistakable tang of envy and crawled beside the cabin's wooden shell, sliding underneath the windowpane and out of sight.

Another *boom* echoed across the sky, and a large crack sounded directly above her head.

She rolled to her side and tucked her knees to her chest, mud squishing into her brand-new jeans. She followed the sound with her eyes, locking onto the roof where the top half of a tree had divorced its counterpart.

Flipping back to her knees, Maggie scurried to the other end of the cabin. Peering around the corner, she whispered, "Come out, come out wherever you are."

Someone in the universe took her taunting as a challenge because the clouds rolled in, and bolts of lightning scattered, creating flashes of light in the dark. And she swore she heard a disembodied voice whisper, "Watch this."

****

The storm outside raged, and thunder clapped in the cloudy sky.

Halley waited by the window for Jared's return, but dark prevailed. She couldn't see anything past her reflection. Typically, being alone didn't shake her. She'd spent plenty of nights alone while Mark traveled for business, but standing there in the dim lantern light, listening to the trees squeal and creak, frightened her.

Lightning spread like an electric current and struck a tree along the trail.

Halley screamed and jumped back, the burst of blue-and-white light outside the window blinding her. A deafening *crash* hit the roof, and tin whined above her head.

The entire ceiling would cave in if she couldn't remove the weight of whatever had fallen.

She tugged on her boots and grabbed the lantern off the table. Opening the door, she breathed in the scents of damp moss and mud. In her last clean outfit, she stepped out into the storm. Rain assaulted her skin like water balloons, and her face stung from the accuracy.

Being a hero sounded a lot better in theory.

Halley dug her heels into the slick soil, pausing at the top of the steep hill leading to the creek. A small shed sat at the bottom with an aluminum ladder attached to the side. Now the only question was how to get down the hill without pulling a Jack and Jill. A sit and scoot might be her only option.

She planted herself firmly in the mud and kept the lantern elevated with her splinted arm, digging into the soft ground to gain traction. All her muscles coiled as she scooched slowly down, her boot heels yanking chunks of dirt and grass from the earth.

Halley gasped as the land beneath her feet crumbled, sending her into a full roll toward the bottom.

Pain shot through her forehead. She touched her temple and rubbed the blood on her jeans. Just what she needed, more injuries. Rising to her knees, she steadied herself against the shed's sturdy frame. She patted the ground for her lantern but only found shattered bits.

Heat settled in her cheeks, and her throat ached from holding back tears. Letting them fall was something the old Halley would do. She didn't need saving. She just needed to stand tall and finish what she started.

Feeling around the shed's rough-cut sides, she located the ladder and lifted the aluminum frame from the rungs. She stood at the bottom and looked up. Getting back would be difficult, and gravity and Mother

Nature would be working against her. Darkness blanketed the land, but she caught a glimpse of the layout when the lightning lit up the night sky.

And she had a plan.

Halley pressed the ladder's feet into the mud, gently easing the edges flat to the ground. After securing her makeshift bridge, she climbed up. When she reached the end of the ladder, she repeated her previous motions and climbed all over again until she reached the top.

She rolled onto her back and cried, soaking in her accomplishment. Her arm had started to swell again, but she didn't care. Without Mark, without Jared, without anyone, she made it. For the first time in her adult life, she stood on her own two feet and depended on no one.

Leaning her aluminum helper against the porch rail, Halley stepped inside to find a new lantern. Floorboards by the table creaked, sending a shot of panic into her throat. Instinctively, she shifted to the dark corner of the living room. "Is someone there? Jared, is that you?"

"Well, you're half right. Someone's here, but it isn't Jared, honey."

The low, raspy voice sent a chill down her spine. Halley hadn't heard the familiar tone in a long time, but the unique, salty bitch pitch was impossible to mistake. "Maggie? What are you doing here? How did you find me?" Her hands trembled, but not from the cold.

"I didn't have to *find* you. I knew you were here all along."

Maggie's face illuminated as she struck the match, a ball of orange-and-red flames collecting at the end.

She trailed along the table, lighting candles one by one until she came chest to chest with Halley. The corner of her lips curled into a malicious grin.

Nausea mingled with the already maxed-out panic brewing in Halley's stomach. She stepped back and forced some space between them, using the table. "I-I don't understand. You knew about the cabin?"

"So naïve, Halley. Where do you think Mark brought me when we made love?"

That explained the rumpled sheets. Honestly, it explained almost everything. Halley shook her head, droplets of water falling to the floor from the ends of her hair. Maggie couldn't possibly be stupid enough to believe she was special—that she had an all-access, exclusive pass to this den of lies. Time for a reality check.

With a smile and a snort, Halley happily addressed the elephant in the room. "I'm naïve? You're dumber than I thought if you think you're the only one Mark brought up here." Her confidence soared as she stepped forward. The air she created between them wafted a peculiar scent into her nostrils—peppermint and a hint of eucalyptus.

The revelation wasn't funny, but she couldn't help but laugh. "Let me ask you something, Mags. Do you wear vanilla perfume? That's not what I'm smelling from over here."

"Where are you going with this little scratch-and-sniff question?"

"I just wondered, because when I arrived and lay on *my* pillow, the only thing I could smell was vanilla. Don't get me wrong, you may be willing to switch things up now and then, but you don't strike me as a perfume whore. Now, I'm no private detective, so why don't you take a moment, think things over, and tell me what that means to you?"

Maggie's hand disappeared behind her back momentarily before bringing a large kitchen knife to the forefront. She rolled the knife's blade in the candle flame, and Halley's confidence faded.

"Hmm. It probably means you should learn how to keep your mouth shut."

The woman had a valid point. A normal, sane person would avoid pissing off someone holding a knife whose intentions were most likely to maim—or kill. Halley swallowed the golf ball-sized lump in her throat. She was sick of being silenced. Her whole life had revolved around being seen and not heard.

Tonight, she'd be loud.

"You're the one then, huh? You killed Mark."

Devilish laughter rang out into the dimly lit space. "I would have gotten away with it too. Everything was going according to plan, but you just had to run off after the car accident, didn't you? If you'd stayed put, I wouldn't be here right now."

"And what plan would that be? You're gonna have to elaborate on your mastermind scheme, because I'm not sure I understand."

"Oh, you know. I drug you and Mark. Then I kill him. When the cops find you next to his dead body unharmed, you get a life sentence for his murder, I get the revenge I've been craving, and you get to learn how to make toilet wine. Sounds like a win-win to me."

Halley had to bow. Maggie had thought the first part out well. If that truck hadn't plowed into them, Halley would be looking down the barrel of life behind bars. "Ah, yes. Drugging the wine was clever, I'll give you that. But I have to know…how did you manage to get the drug into the wine?"

Maggie smoothed out her shirt, looking unnervingly proud of her elaborate plan. "How?"

"Pretty sure that's what I asked."

"Quick and easy. I bought the wine, shoved a needle full of sedatives down into the cork, and gave the bottle to Mark as kind of a peace offering after he broke things off with me. When you were distracted after finding him the next morning, I tiptoed in and snatched the glasses off your table. Honestly, I thought you'd catch me in the act, and the adrenaline rush was kind of thrilling in a way."

"So when I heard the screen door slam, that was you? You were at my house watching everything." Halley snorted. "You are a clever little tramp, aren't you? Sick and twisted too."

"You're one to talk. You seem to be moving on nice and fast after just losing your husband to a *deranged* murderer."

Maggie's face contorted in the uneven light, making her look monstrous. Or maybe the light just showed her true colors. Halley hadn't known the woman long before Maggie married her loser ex-husband and moved away, but not in a million years would she have suspected the red-haired, hometown beauty of being a scheming, murderous bitch. "Yeah, well, it's not like I could've been with Mark after he tainted himself with the town trash."

"Keep talking, wench." Maggie grinned and growled simultaneously, taking a full stride forward. "Your time is just about up."

Halley lifted a hand. "Wait, wait. I just have one more question."

Maggie sighed and rolled her eyes. "I suppose I could allow one more question before I kill you."

Come on, Halley. Think. Think.

She had to drag their conversation out long enough to come up with a plan or, at the very least, until Jared came back. "Why did you kill Mark? I mean, okay, obviously you two were having an affair, but if you were so in love with him, why would you want to end his life? If you went through all this trouble just because of an affair, then you're just a petty priss with some seriously low self-esteem. Tell me, *Mags*. What really pushed you over the edge?"

Loud chiming from the table heightened Halley's dread. And only being able to hear one side of the conversation didn't help ease the fear.

Maggie lowered her voice. "Hello? Wonderful…oh, yes." She licked her lips at Halley like she planned to eat her for dinner. "I'm here with her now.

The phone beeped. "Let's wait until our other guests arrive, shall we? I promise, I'll explain everything."

****

Jared braced himself against the old white door separating the complex apartments. Breathing in deep to steady himself, he mentally and physically prepared for what might go down. Bo was injured but still outweighed Jared by at least seventy-five pounds and had him by half a head in height. There was no point in pretending he'd win in a fistfight with Bo because the expectation was unrealistic at best.

Knock, knock. "Bo? Are you in there? Answer the door!" He rapped again.

More silence.

Jared twisted the handle, and the door pushed open. "Bo?" Drawing his gun, he listened for signs of life, and every hair on his body stood at attention. The wallpaper was tattered and dingy, and pieces fell to the ground as he slid his back along the wall.

This place went beyond the definition of a dump. Buckets overflowing with rainwater lined the living room, and Jared's eyes watered when the pungent smell of mold filled his nostrils. A rat would take one look around and check out. No wonder Bo always asked for a rolling drop-off when his truck wasn't running. Jared would never have let him live here had he known the conditions.

Zip.

Jared froze and held his breath.

Zip. Someone was pulling a zipper down the dilapidated hallway—last room on the left.

He peeked through the cracked door and saw feet passing by in constant motion. A rotted floorboard gave under his step, stopping all movement. He kicked the door open, his nose connecting with the barrel of Bo's gun.

"Should've known you'd show up eventually." Bo kept his pistol aimed at Jared's head.

"Why did you leave the hospital?" Jared cringed. Bo was pale and hunched over, barely the man he knew. "You look like hell."

A half-smile inched up the corner of Bo's mouth. "I didn't have a choice. Someone's trying to kill me, and once Captain Maxwell finds out about what I did, he'll take my badge. This job is all I have left."

Jared could relate. The captain would take his badge too if he ever found out about how Jared hid Halley from the system. Honestly, he'd be in deeper shit than Bo. "Just put the gun down. We can work through this together. Running away is only going to make things worse." He lowered his gun, but Bo only tightened his grip around the trigger.

"Things can't get any worse! I have someone out there hunting me like an animal, I'm gonna be fired and put in jail for blackmail, and I have nowhere left to turn. I need to get out of town before whoever wants to put a bullet in my head finds me and succeeds." Bo lowered his gun, letting it fall to his side. "I never meant for anyone to get hurt, I swear."

"That's what happens when you make a stupid plan and don't think things through…people get hurt. But what I don't get is why someone would be trying to kill you. You said all you did was give Mark a stack of photos, right?"

Bo stepped back to the bed and sat. "Yeah. I mean, I threatened to tell his wife about the affairs, but I never laid a hand on him."

"Were the ones you gave him originals? Were they the only ones you have?"

Leaning back, Bo reached into a side zipper and pulled out a small memory card. "I only printed out the ones that didn't show their faces. You know, out of respect and all. But I have hundreds of photos on this card…among other things. Feel free to check it out. Maybe there's something in there you can use, but I'm leaving."

Jared flashed to the night he circled back to the

crime scene. The masked person he'd grappled with was looking for those photos—the ones he found in the grandfather clock. Even if the images weren't of their faces, there could've been an incriminating birthmark or tattoo—something out of the ordinary that could point them out to police.

"Well, Bo, someone out there knows about you. They know what you did, and they most likely know you have something they don't want the world to see." Jared lifted Bo's bags over his shoulders. "Come on. We have to go. Do you remember if any of the women had any distinguishing marks?"

Bo nodded, swaying as he stood. "One girl had an elf tattooed on her butt—that was weird. Most of them had moles in some place or another, but one woman had a unique-looking mark on the back of her neck. It sorta looked like a firework."

Jared swallowed hard, saliva sticking to his throat like cement. "A firework?"

"Yep. Pretty big too. I wonder how she ended up with it?"

Jared held the door open with his foot. "I know exactly how she was marked, but what I don't know is how I missed what was right in front of my face."

****

The car door opened, squeaking from lack of oil.

Jared threw Bo's bags in the back and picked up the envelope of pictures, lifting them out one by one. None of them bore the firework he'd been searching for. He ripped the front of the envelope down the center. There, stuck to the backside, was the scar—the scar he'd given Maggie on her tenth birthday.

She had warned them over and over not to piss

with the firecrackers, but what ten-year-old boy listened to a ten-year-old girl? He ran the lighter across his jeans and watched the flame ignite the fuse.

Maggie was too close.

A firecracker escaped from the pod and landed on the back of her neck. She ignored him for at least a month. When she wore her hair in a ponytail, guilt bit down on him.

"Bo, you ready?" Jared shifted his gaze over the hood.

Bo stood with his hands in the air, and a gun pointed at his side.

"Cordini?"

"Get in the car, Jared," Cordini ordered.

"And if I don't?"

Cordini shoved the pistol deeper into Jared's partner's ribs, and Bo grimaced. "Park is pretty full tonight, and they got a great band to play. I'd hate to see a bunch of innocent people get hurt because you couldn't follow directions."

"All right, all right." Jared slowly reached for his weapon.

Cordini raised his gun to Bo's temple. "Throw your weapon in the car and move."

Jared tossed his gun onto the front seat before following the man to his squad car.

After pinning Jared's wrists behind him, the mama's boy extraordinaire zip-tied them. "There. Let's see you squirm your way out of those." Cordini laughed and smacked the back of Jared's head. He opened the back door to the squad car. "Get in."

Jared growled but slid into the back seat.

Cordini slammed the car door and walked around

the back before opening the other door.

Jared caught Bo in his lap seconds later.

A bright-red splotch seeped through the front of Bo's white T-shirt.

"Cordini, you moron. He's about to bleed to death. We have to get him back to the hospital."

Chuckling, Cordini slammed the door shut and got into the driver's seat. "That's not my problem. Besides, if he dies, then there's no one left to talk—besides you, of course, and that other chick. But don't worry, Maggie will take care of her."

Jared brought himself to the edge of his seat and slammed his shoulder into the divider. "When I get my hands on you, and I will, I'm gonna choke you to death with my bare hands."

Cordini smiled and glanced in the rearview mirror. "Relax, boys. We're goin' to a party."

Bo nudged Jared with his shoulder, his face whiter than snow in December. "Do you smell a rat?"

Rat was too kind a name for what Stan Cordini really was.

Chapter Fourteen

The cabin door flew open. Jared and Bo shuffled in, hands out of sight and a gun pointed at their backs.

Halley didn't recognize the man whose finger was wrapped around the trigger, holding on for dear life.

"Jared!" Halley stepped forward to grab him—to hold him in her arms, but the firm grasp around her wrist stopped her. "Thank God you're alive."

Jared soldiered to her defense, but the uniform kicked him behind the knee and threw both men to the covered couch. How had she not noticed? The man in the uniform was a cop. He had to be—unless he got the uniform from a costume shop. But the badge looked real, the metal glaring when hit by the candlelight.

Frustration oozed through Jared's expression, and now she knew why. Dirty cops weren't exactly invited to the precinct Christmas party.

"Doesn't feel so good being kicked in the leg, now does it, Jared?" Maggie said, tightening her grip on Halley's arm.

The knife's point put pressure on the center of Halley's spine, digging into her skin, poking through her wet shirt like it was chiffon.

Maggie glared at Bo. "You should be dead, Officer Frazer. I'm less than thrilled to see you're still breathing. You know, minding your own business would've been the smart thing to do. Everyone would still be alive had you just dealt with your trauma like a normal person. But, no. You just have to go around, issuing ultimatums that weren't yours to dish out."

"Fuck you." Bo gritted his teeth. "You don't know anything about me."

"Oh, no? Let me think. Poor abandoned Boden couldn't get over his sister's death, so he decided to be a big man and use blackmail. Last time I checked that's illegal, isn't it, Stan?"

"Sure is." Cordini laughed.

"See? I know more about you than you think."

"I don't understand, Mags," Jared spoke softly. "This isn't you. I've known you my entire life. What happened?"

Maggie's shrill laugh reverberated across the bare cabin walls. "You people with all your questions. If you'd shut the hell up, I'd tell you."

Shuddering as the knife grazed the back of her neck, Halley closed her eyes. At this point, the anticipation of imminent death might be worse than dying.

"Well," Maggie mused. "After my divorce, sweet, sweet Mark was the only one who came to comfort me in my time of need. Seems he took his role as a knight in shining armor a little too seriously. Falling in love with him wasn't my intention, but you know the saying, *The heart wants what the heart wants.* Unfortunately, our hearts didn't want the same thing."

"You killed him because he didn't love you?" Halley wriggled free and faced the woman who tried to steal her freedom. The woman who killed a man in cold blood, leaving her to hold the bag. "Pretty high-school-revenge plot, don't you think, Mags?"

"Depends on your definition." Maggie's hot breath fogged up the blade as she vigorously rubbed the edge with her shirt. "I gave him my whole heart. I stayed his mistress for six months. I wanted to have his babies. I was *supposed* to have his babies!"

His babies. Suzanne. All the burning questions finally fizzled out. "You killed Suzanne Akers too."

"I had a little help." Maggie pointed the knife toward the cop and shrugged.

"I took care of her." Cordini smiled smugly. "Maggie said we could be together if I got rid of Suzanne. See, she found out about Maggie and that guy. If she blabbed, then we'd never get to be together. Maggie wanted her baby too, so we're gonna kidnap the thing and raise her together."

"Shut up, Stan!" Maggie shouted. "God. No wonder everyone on the force hates you, you blathering idiot."

"You gonna let her talk to you like that, Cordini?" Jared taunted. "Mama's boy can't stand up for himself?"

"Screw you, Jared! You don't know what you're talking about."

Bo chimed in. "Yeah, Jared, didn't you know Cordini's whipped."

Cordini put his gun to Jared's head. "I am *not* whipped!"

"Stan!" Maggie scolded. "Can't you see that they're just trying to get a rise out of you?"

Maggie stalked over to Halley and dug her sharp, jagged nails deep into Halley's forearm, pulling her closer. "I swear, if you want something done right, you just need to do it yourself." She stuck the blade to

Halley's back. "If you idiots don't knock your crap off, I'll kill her."

Jared made one last retort. "Hey, Cordini, your safety is on."

Halley watched the next scene unfold as if they were moving in slow motion.

As Stan looked down, Jared looped his hands under his feet to the front and grabbed Cordini's hands, emptying his clip into the ceiling.

The tree. Halley had forgotten all about the tree on the roof.

The metal groaned.

"Jared, move!"

An enormous chunk of tree, limbs and all, crashed through the ceiling, pinning Cordini to the floor.

Mother Nature sent her a masterpiece after all.

For a moment, a sense of safety washed over her. They were going to get out alive, and her name would be cleared—no longer tarnished by a murder she didn't commit.

Halley opened her mouth, but words wouldn't come out.

A sharp pain ripped through her back and into her chest. She sucked in breath after breath, but her lungs never seemed satisfied. Voices swirled as her knees hit the floor, the loud thud echoing in her ears. She gasped when the blade left her flesh. The world spun while numbness enveloped her body on the wet wood floor. She watched Jared's mouth move. He screamed at her, but his face blurred, and her vision dimmed.

Okay. Maybe *she* wasn't going to survive. She had to stay awake to tell Jared she loved him one final time. He needed to know how the past few days had changed her—given her hope for the future. She didn't have much time.

****

Jared left the floor in a bounding leap, catching Maggie off guard when he pummeled her to the ground.

The knife flew from her hands, landing at Bo's feet.

"Bo, grab the knife!"

Bo leaned down and moaned. "Got the knife."

"Good, now cut my zip ties first, and then I'll get yours."

Bo laid the sharp blade on the edge of the tie and swiped up.

Accepting the knife, Jared returned the favor. "Get to Halley now! Is she breathing?"

"Her pulse is weak, Jared. I don't know if she'll pull through." He placed his hand on her back to cover the wound. "She's losing a lot of blood."

Jared tore the phone from Maggie's pocket and slid it to Bo. "Call 911 and tell them to home in on the tracking device in Cordini's cruiser. That will be easier than trying to explain the location." He turned back to his captive. "What have you done, Mags?"

"I did what I had to. You'll never understand what it's like loving someone so much you'd do anything to keep them, only to find out they never really loved you back. How could he do this to me? How could he have a baby with another woman when he knew that was all I ever wanted?" She squirmed beneath him as he held her wrists against the hard slabs.

Jared looked into the eyes of a woman he'd known since childhood and saw nothing but hatred and pain. "What happened to you, Maggie?"

"Life happened to me. A person can only take so much before the dark they hold inside boils to the surface." She laughed and screeched like a feral animal. "Mark just lit the fuse."

Placing his weight evenly, he slipped off his belt and secured the strap around her wrists. Maggie fought hard, but he overpowered her.

Jared turned his head in Halley's direction.

Blood pooled in a perfect circle, stretching out like a river under her back.

He took off his shirt. "Hold this over the wound. We have to control the bleeding until the medics get here."

Maggie's thrashing and screams were something straight out of a horror film, almost like she was possessed. "I hope she dies, and I hope you live a miserable, lonely life, you callous son of a bitch."

Jared ignored her, kneeling at Halley's side. Her eyes were open and full of fear, but she said nothing. He'd seen that look many times before…she was in shock. He would give his life to take her pain away—to inflict the wound upon himself if hers would heal. "Halley, don't worry, I'm right here."

Halley's chest heaved. Her gaze met Bo's. "I'm s-s-sorry about L-Lanie."

Bo lowered his head. "This is all my fault. You have no reason to be sorry. Just save your breath and don't talk anymore. You'll be all right."

She moved her eyes back to Jared, her breathing more labored and subtle.

She was fading, and there wasn't anything he could do to save her. He placed his lips on her mouth, and her body shuddered beneath him. "I love you, Halley. You have to hold on. Please, I need you to stay with me."

She placed a hand gently on his face and nodded. As her mouth opened, her hand dropped to the floor, and her eyelids slid shut.

Jared held her for a moment, watching shallow breaths move her chest up and down.

Bo sat beside them, barely hanging on, the front of his shirt covered in red.

Death and destruction surrounded Jared. Was this what he signed up for? Would staying in this line of work always cause so much hurt?

Maybe he never noticed the dark before Halley, but losing her tonight would kill a part of him too. He'd always stayed back and played it safe, never letting anyone get too close. All his greatest fears had just come to pass in an instant, and there was nothing he could do to stop it. What kind of hero did that make him? He'd sworn to serve and protect. He might have served, but he failed to protect. He screwed up by not taking her in when he found her. This wouldn't be happening if he'd done his job.

Ten minutes passed. Still no ambulance. "Bo, she's going to die."

Bo stood and wobbled over to Cordini, still out cold under a wad of tree. He unclipped the keys from the rat's belt and tossed them to Jared. "Go, and I'll stay here with these two."

"No. I can't. They won't be able to find you. They're tracking his car, remember? Plus, look at you. You can barely stand."

"Oooh." Maggie sang from the floor. "Maybe I'll get two for the price of one today."

"Shut the hell up, Maggie. I swear to God if she

dies, I'll kill you myself." The devilish laugh put his soul on ice.

"Talk, talk, talk. You don't have the balls to kill me. You'd lose everything."

Jared pressed his shirt harder against the wound. "I have nothing left to lose." Cradling Halley's head, he lifted her off the floor and pressed her body to his chest. "Are you sure you'll be okay?"

Bo nodded. "I'll call dispatch and have them track this phone instead. Now, go! Be the hero."

The kick from his boot swung the door open. The rain had stopped, but clouds blocked the moon and stars, leaving him blinded by darkness. Bo's words played on repeat in his head. *Be the hero.* His body ached, his ribs burned, and the last time he'd slept more than three hours was close to a week ago.

His entire system begged him to give up—to call it quits, but heroes never gave up, and officers never surrendered.

Halley's limp body weighed him down, and his feet sank deeper into the mud. He pushed the car alarm button, the blinking lights and sounds guiding him.

Only a few more feet. Come on, Jared, hold out just a little longer.

****

What a mess he'd created. Bo slunk to the couch, yanking down the neck of his shirt to assess the damage. His stitches had torn, and sweat rolled down his face. Nothing but destruction surrounded him. Wasn't this what he'd wanted—to turn Mark's life upside down? He could never have known how many lives would be destroyed due to his inability to let go. Leaving Blackstone was a mistake, and he'd give anything to go back. He would've lived a miserable life, but at least Halley, Jared, Mark, Detective Arnold, and Suzanne might've stood a chance.

"What's the matter, Bo?" Maggie jeered. "Not feeling too hot?"

Bo hoisted his bleeding body off the couch, stepped over Cordini, and flipped Maggie to her back with his boot. "The system shouldn't even waste time on someone like you. Murderers don't deserve three meals a day or a bed to sleep in."

"You're one to talk. Technically, this is all your fault, Officer Frazer. What's that say about you?"

Bo rested his foot on her chest. He could easily end this. His career was already over, and life would never be the same. Metaphorical blood stained his hands. No amount of scrubbing or penance would wash his sins away, so what difference would one more black splotch on his soul make? Pressing down, he watched as Maggie's turquoise eyes bulged, her mouth wide as she gasped for air.

Any more weight, and she'd suffocate.

With a strained voice, Maggie spoke. "See? We aren't so different, after all. The darkness comes for everyone eventually."

Bo lifted his foot, stepping back as lights flashed through the windows. She was right. If he took her life, he'd be no better. His mistakes would cost him dearly, but killing Maggie would strip him of all freedoms, and that was something he wasn't willing to relinquish. "You're a delusional bitch. Death's too good for you."

Captain Maxwell burst through the door, gun drawn, chest covered in Kevlar. "Bo?" He surveyed the room as two other officers split to either side behind him. "What the hell happened here?"

One of the officers reached down, placing two fingers on Cordini's neck. "He's alive, Captain. But his legs look broken. It's gonna take more than the three of us to move this tree."

The other officer lifted Maggie off the floor. She grinned from ear to ear as he walked her out the door.

Bo winced and swayed. "How did you find us?"

"We were almost here when you called dispatch again. You haven't exactly been stealthy, Bo. I've been tagging you for days. Now, you didn't answer my question," Captain Maxwell said, sliding his gun in the holster at his side. "What happened?"

Bo swallowed hard. "If you take me to the hospital, I'll tell you." His knees hit the floor, a small crack in one floorboard the last image his eyes caught before the world faded.

Chapter Fifteen

"Wake up, Halley," a distant voice called, seemingly from out in space. "Come on now, open your eyes. Atta girl."

She managed tiny slits, but the light pouring into her retinas stung like the time she cut an onion and accidentally rubbed her eyes. Fire seared her throat and lungs as she sucked in a deep breath. The cough, though, left her wishing for death.

"Whoa now, settle down. You've had a pretty rough night, and we don't need you blowing out any stitches." The woman's voice was soft, sweet, and sounded exactly like her mother's.

"Who are you? And where am I?"

"My name is Dr. Marilyn Sherell. Do you know what year we are in?"

"Last I checked, 2022. Is this some sort of alternate-reality type thing?"

Dr. Sherell chuckled. "Not that I'm aware of, but hey, you never can tell." She grabbed a clipboard from the end of the bed. "Do you remember what happened?"

Dizziness slapped her across the face as she tried to sit up. Bits and pieces of what happened streamed into her consciousness, but they were chunked and hard to remember. "I got hit by a semi?"

"My, my. We are a funny one, aren't we?"

"I'm just kidding. I think" Halley turned, hiding her eyes from the light. Pain shot up her back, making the rest of her body go rigid. *Oh, yeah.* Her memory came flooding back. "That bitch stabbed me."

"I don't normally condone vulgar language in my hospital, but yes, you were indeed stabbed." Dr. Sherell wrote on the clipboard for a moment before placing two fingers on Halley's wrist. She wrapped a blood pressure cuff around her arm and squeezed the bulb on the end until a small whimper escaped Halley's lips. "You're fortunate to be alive, Mrs. Martin. There were a few times in the operating room when I thought we might lose you."

"Please, just call me Halley." The next time somebody called her Mrs. Martin, it better come after *ex*. After getting released from the hospital, her first plan of action would be a name change. She wanted nothing to do with Mark or any other part of the Martin legacy. They had no children together, and nothing he owned was in her name…a clean break would be easy.

"Anyway, Halley, you came in with a punctured lung and profound blood loss. If that nice officer hadn't taken such good care of you, I don't think you'd be lying here right now."

Holy stromboli. "Where is Jared? I mean, Officer Collins? Please tell me he's okay."

She nodded. "He's fine. Officer Collins stepped out for a cup of coffee. He's barely left your side since you came in. Loyalty like that is hard to find."

Didn't she know it.

Dr. Sherell slipped Halley's chart back into the wire basket, patted her foot, and handed her a heart-shaped pillow. "I'll go see if I can find your hero while you get some rest. Oh, and when you feel another coughing fit coming on, squeeze this to cushion some of the jarring motions."

"Thanks, Dr. Sherell."

"Please, call me Marilyn," she said, slipping behind the curtain and disappearing into the hall.

A knock on the glass door startled her. There was no possible way Marilyn found Jared that fast. "Come in." Halley cleared the scratch from her throat.

"Can I get you some water?" Bo wheeled around the bed, found a cup, and lifted the straw to her lips.

The room-temperature water tasted like chlorine, but her throat no longer felt as dry as the Sahara. "Thanks, I appreciate the help."

"I wish I could do more." Bo shifted his wheelchair to the side and sighed. "I just wanted to tell you how sorry I am for everything you went through because of me. Maggie was right about what she said at the cabin. If I'd just stayed out of Mark's life or dealt with Lanie's death like a normal person, everyone would still be alive."

"Being normal is vastly overrated." Halley beckoned him closer and laid a hand over his. "I remember the day you took the stand in court to testify. You were so young and scared. I remember silently praying for you—hoping that after the trial ended, you would be okay. I wish those prayers had been answered, but we can't live in the past." She had learned her lesson the hard way over the past few days. She gripped his hand harder. "There are no dead-ends in life because the choice to turn around and take a different path is always available."

His eyes glistened. "Can you forgive me?"

"If forgiveness will help you move on, then yes, I forgive you. But I think the real question is whether or not you can forgive yourself."

"Maybe, in time." Bo kissed the back of her hand and wheeled himself out of the room.

Halley's thoughts shifted to Mark as she leaned back against the pillow. Forgiveness is easy to give if the person handing out the betrayal isn't someone you promised to spend the rest of your life with. Forgiving someone she barely knew…simple. Forgiving someone she built a home with… not so much. But like Bo, that would come with time.

****

"Goddamned coffee machine." Jared kicked the corner and shook the sides. "Who needs caffeine, anyway?"

"Um, Officer Collins?"

Jared turned to find Halley's doctor watching him, seemingly amused. "Sorry, It's been a long night. Day?" He swatted at the machine again. "I don't even know what I'm working with at this point."

"Understandable." She reassured him, sticking a nickel into the machine and pressing two buttons. "It's Saturday at 6:00 in the morning. Also, I promise the machine works very well when you put the right amount of change in."

He cringed. The cup slid into the holders, rocking as liquid rose to the rim. "How is she?" He retrieved the steaming cup from Dr. Sherell's hands.

"Honestly, she's kind of snarky. But in an alive sort of way. Basing my prognosis on that alone, I'd say she's going to be fine. She'll be sore for quite a while, but fine."

"She's awake?" Coffee overflow splashed onto his hand, burning a finger or two. He winced. Scenario after scenario had played out in his imagination while he waited for her surgery to end. What if she didn't make it? What if the knife had hit just right and she woke up paralyzed? It wouldn't have mattered if she came out of the operating room with six legs—as long as she came out alive, nothing else mattered.

She smiled. "If you're not careful, you might end up in the hospital bed next to her. But, yes, she's awake and asking for you."

Jared wanted to hug the older woman with her black-and-gray speckled hair. Hell, if he could be sure she wouldn't deck him, he'd kiss her. In one night, she'd stitched up his partner and saved the love of his life. "Thanks, Doc. I owe you one."

"How about you stop beating on the machines around here? You do that, and I'll call us even."

Jared sucked down some coffee, stifling a yelp from the burn. "I think I can manage to direct my outbursts elsewhere."

Dr. Sherell walked away, disappearing behind a set of double doors just as Bo wheeled around the corner. "Hey, have you heard the good news? Halley's awake."

"Yeah. The doctor said she was asking for me." Jared peered into his cup.

"Well, aren't you gonna go in and see her?"

All charges against Halley had been dropped, and part of him worried that things between them would be different. She didn't need him to save her anymore. Would she still want him? Jared groaned. "What if Halley realizes she doesn't really love me? I don't think I can go in there and face her right now."

193

"Okay, but if you don't go in, you're just going to spend the rest of your life moping around, wondering what might've happened had you stopped being a giant baby and gone in. So, save yourself the mental agony and get your ass in there."

Jared chuckled. "Well, when you put it so eloquently." He tossed his cup toward the trash can and made a three-pointer. "Before I go...how are you holding up?"

Bo patted his chest. "All stitched up like new and raring to go."

"You know that's not what I meant."

"I know, I know. I told the captain everything." Bo shrugged. "I'm suspended until a proper investigation has been conducted, but I'm not holding my breath on ever getting my job back. I made my bed, and now I have to lie in it."

Jared nodded. He had respect for anyone who could admit their mistakes and pay their due time. Idiots who never took responsibility were the ones who fried his bacon. "So, what are your plans now?"

"Well, I called a buddy of mine back home, and he's renting me space in a building he's selling. Not sure what I'll do for money yet, but I'll figure something out. I always do."

"Isn't that like three hours away?" Jared put more money into the coffee machine—the correct amount this time—and pressed the buttons Dr. Sherell had shown him, then handed Bo the cup.

"Yeah. But I've been thinking, and maybe some distance isn't such a bad thing." Swinging the chair around, Bo gestured to the double doors. "Now quit stalling and go see your girl."

Now or never, Jared. Now or never.
****

She looked peaceful and content under the thick white hospital sheet. A nice shade of rose pink painted her cheeks like a ceramic doll's. He stepped back, unwilling to wake her after everything she'd been through, but his clumsy effort and a metal chair had other plans.

"Jared? Are you there?" Sleep laced her tone.

"Yeah, Halley, I'm right here." Placing the malicious chair by her side, he kissed her knuckles. "How're you feeling?"

"Tired and sore, but I think I'll live."

Jared braced himself for her answer to his next question. "Halley, I—"

She cut him off and squeezed his arm. "Am I gonna go to jail?"

He couldn't help but laugh at her innocence. "No. Cordini overshared like usual. Maggie will be going away for a long, long time, and your name has officially been cleared." He tucked a rogue hair behind her ear. "Halley, I need to know how you feel about me. About us?"

"You mean, do I still love you?"

Sweat beaded across his forehead, and he lowered his gaze. Jesus. Chasing down criminals didn't even have this effect on him. "Yeah. I mean, sometimes, during times of stress or trauma, people form false feelings for whoever is helping them. Is that what's happening here, with us?"

"Okay, number one, unless you have a license to do so, don't you dare *shrink* me. Number two, don't you ever accuse me of having false feelings. And number three, I'm so in love with you I can't see straight. I want to spend the rest of my life with you. Jared, I love you."

His eyes must have glazed over. Either that or his heart literally stopped beating for a split second because Halley grabbed him by the face, said something about stupidity, and kissed him like he was the last man on earth.

Halley's eyes sparkled. "Did you hear me? I said I love you."

Jared pressed his lips hard against hers, drinking in everything about her—from the way she tasted to her scent. He pulled back. "I heard what you said, but I wanted to hear you say it one more time."

She swatted at his hand. "You know, you're kind of a jerk."

"The kind of jerk you would want to marry someday?"

Halley held up a finger. "Someday. On one condition."

Jared spread rapid-fire kisses over every inch of Halley's exposed skin. "Anything you want."

"I want to be a mother." Halley grabbed his face, halting the kisses. "And I want to be a mother soon."

"Hal, I'm more than happy to give my all in the baby-making department, but making a baby doesn't always happen immediately."

"Well, maybe I don't want a baby in the traditional sense." She scratched underneath his chin. "Do you catch my drift?"

He did. He caught her hint all the way from third-floor maternity. "Are you sure this is what you want?"

"More than anything."

Halley's smile cut into his hardened heart. Even if he'd tried to resist, he would've failed miserably. "Fine, but you have to fill out all the paperwork."

Halley laughed, grabbed him by the shirt, and pulled him close. "Yes, Officer Collins. I'll do all the dirty work."

"But…" He trailed off.

"But what?"

"What if I break your heart?"

Halley laid his hand on her chest. "What if you fix it?"

Chapter Sixteen

The year had passed before Halley's eyes, and the way she viewed life was nothing more than a remnant of how she used to see things. She'd held onto worries, fears, and slights that kept her stationary—never allowing her to be free. She'd rarely used the freedoms life permitted, which was ironic considering she desperately feared losing them. But not anymore.

The bailiff bellowed from the corner of the stand. "All rise for the honorable Judge Elizabeth Gates."

Halley and Jared rose from their seats, waiting for Judge Gates to take hers.

Halley was grateful for the chance to stretch her legs. Their case was over an hour late, and her butt had gone numb from sitting on the paisley upholstered seats. Above their heads, a bulb in the antique chandelier flickered. The rollercoaster ride was almost over.

"Mr. and Mrs. Collins, I am so happy to see you again." Judge Gates smiled and adjusted her robe. Gray hairs framed her round face. "Today is the big day." The plump woman waved her hand. "You may be seated."

Halley's leg bounced under the table. This moment was the one keeping them moving. "It is, Your Honor, and we've been waiting since last fall."

Judge Gates flipped through a stack of papers on

her desk. "Yes, I'm well aware of how long you've been waiting, Mrs. Collins." She brushed something off her sleeve. "You folks have run into some speed bumps along the way."

"Yes, Your Honor."

"Now, let's get down to business, shall we?"

Halley nodded and smiled, squeezing Jared's hand. This was surreal. Her heart pounded, and the tightness in her throat worsened.

"We are here today for twelve-month-old Lanie Akers. Is the paternal grandmother still petitioning for custody?"

Halley bit her lip. "No, Your Honor. She will no longer be petitioning for custody."

"Is there a reason for her withdrawal?"

Mark's mother, Beth, had spent the last year doing everything in her power to make Halley's life a living hell, starting with denying her entry to Mark's funeral. As his wife, she had a right to pay her respects…but Beth Martin didn't feel the same way.

After she and Jared had completed their foster parent training and received their clearances, Beth caught wind of their plans to adopt Lanie. Child Services had already given the woman the chance to take in her son's child, but she refused, claiming Lanie wasn't Mark's.

Lanie had his eyes—gray with specks of blue, like an approaching storm.

When Halley looked into them, sometimes Mark's face appeared.

The day after Halley and Jared took Lanie into their home, Beth halted the adoption process by seeking full custody. It seemed one of the caseworkers told her hairdresser about the small-town scandal, and the hairdresser happened to be Mark's cousin, Lorraine.

Halley barely had enough restraint to keep herself from slapping the dentures right out of Beth's mouth.

"Yes," Jared chimed in. "Beth Martin had a heart attack last week and sadly passed away."

Adjusting her glasses, Judge Gates met his gaze. "I'm sorry to hear that. Is there any other grandparent or biological family member who might object to this adoption?"

"No, Your Honor. Lanie's biological maternal grandparents have made their wishes for no contact very clear. They have no interest in forging a relationship with her. And her paternal grandfather passed away years ago." Halley kissed the top of Lanie's head and breathed in her scent. Baby soap and strawberries.

Lanie stared up at Halley, her beauty melting any ounce of fear Halley'd been carrying.

Jared leaned over and pecked Lanie on the cheek. Resting his hand on Halley's knee, he pressed her leg to the floor. "Can you stop shaking your leg? It's like someone let a jackhammer loose in here."

"Sorry," she whispered. "I'm just really nervous. I don't want any more surprises."

His grip on her knee softened. "I know you're scared, but I promise, everything is going to work out, okay?"

Halley nodded. "I love you."

"I love you both more than you'll ever know."

Judge Gates cleared her throat. "Is there something you two would like to share with the courtroom?"

"No. Sorry, Your Honor." Jared laced his fingers

together and laid them on the table.

"Well, then. If there are no further interruptions, I would like to close out this case." The judge raised her gavel. "Mr. and Mrs. Collins, I hereby state that in the case of twelve-month-old Lanie Akers, you will now be her legal guardians for life." She rapped the gavel on the sounding block and smiled. "You will be responsible for her care and growth, along with meeting her every need. You are now her parents, and you will act as such. Congratulations. Court adjourned."

Halley's heart jumped. "You hear that, baby girl?" She lifted Lanie into the air, rejoicing in the beauty of *her* child. "You're officially a Collins."

Jared wrapped his arms around them both. "What do you mean she's officially a Collins? She's been a Collins since the day we brought her home. We didn't need a piece of paper to know she was ours."

Bringing Lanie close, Halley whispered in her ear, "I knew you were mine the first time I laid eyes on you through the nursery window. I will love you forever, Lanie Collins. Let's go home."

A word about the author…

I am a coffee drinking, book-loving, Tourette-having, tattoo-addicted stay-at-home mom. I am a full-time college student pursuing a bachelor's degree in psychology for child and adolescent development.

I live in a small backwoods town with my husband, our daughter, and two dogs who think my furniture is their bed. I started writing at the beginning of the pandemic to stave off the boredom thanks to being quarantined and loved it so much I just never stopped.

http://dmgrantauthor.com

Thank you for purchasing
this publication of The Wild Rose Press, Inc.

For questions or more information
contact us at
info@thewildrosepress.com.

The Wild Rose Press, Inc.
www.thewildrosepress.com

www.ingramcontent.com/pod-product-compliance
Lightning Source LLC
Chambersburg PA
CBHW070500260626
47161CB00004B/1387